THE TRUTH ABOUT LYING

A BIG MOUNTAIN CHRISTMAS NOVEL

CRYSTAL FERRY

FERRY TAIL PUBLISHING LLC

This novel is a work of fiction. Names, characters, places, and incidents are either a product of the author's imagination or are used fictitiously. Any resemblance to actual persons, living or dead, businesses, events, or locales is entirely coincidental.

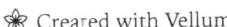

For my mom, who loved this book the most

.

et yourself together, Clara.

The opening chords of a song crept out of the sanctuary and into the ladies' room. Where I was hiding. And crying.

I was supposed to be in my seat. Smiling. Singing. But instead, I sat in a stall wishing I could be somewhere else.

Some*one* else.

God, give me the strength to get through another Sunday morning.

I brushed the tears away, hoping they hadn't ruined the makeup I'd spent nearly an hour applying. I stepped out of the stall and almost ran right into one of my favorite little girls.

"Are you crying, Miss Clara?" she asked.

I thought I was alone.

"Why aren't you in children's church, Emma?" I crouched in front of her so we were eye to eye.

"I can't get my bow back in my hair." She held the pink

bow out in front of her. It was mangled and crushed from her attempts. "It came out when I took off my parka."

"May I help?"

She nodded.

"Were *you* crying, Emma?" I asked as I slipped the bow around her ponytail.

"I tried not to," she said, tears still in her eyes.

"Can I tell you a secret?"

Her eyes widened. "Yes."

"I was crying too," I said. "It's okay to cry."

"I love you, Miss Clara," she said, wrapping her tiny arms around my waist.

"And I love you, Miss Emma." I squeezed her. "Your bow looks perfect. Now let's get you to children's church."

She stood on her tiptoes to look over the counter into the mirror before skipping out of the bathroom.

I placed a hand on my heart. If I ever had children, I'd want them to be just like her.

The sanctuary lights buzzed overhead.

"Thank you, Jesus," Sydney sang from the stage.

The fire alarm beeped behind me.

"You are so good to us." Maybe God was good to her with her glowing skin that made it look like she'd just returned from the Caribbean. My skin was pale, cracked, and dry like a proper Coloradan's should be in the winter.

Sweat beaded on my forehead and rolled down my

back. The heat was cranked to make up for the cold, snowy day.

"We are nothing without you, Lord."

How long are you going to sing-pray, *Sydney*? My feet were starting to hurt in these heels.

Finally, the music ended with Sydney staring up at the ceiling, arms raised in surrender.

People all around me cheered like they were at a concert.

Praise the Lord.

"You may be seated," my husband walked onto the stage in his khaki pants and blue button-down shirt. His blond hair was gelled into little spikes on top of his head, his beard trimmed to perfection. If only everyone knew how much time he spent primping that morning.

I did my best to smile. People watched me almost as intently as they watched him, just waiting for me to make a mistake.

"Today we're going to talk about forgiveness. Please take out your Bibles and turn to Colossians."

Filmy pages crinkled and cracked around me as everyone raced to be the first to find the verse. I pulled out my phone and typed it into my Bible app. Who needed to carry the actual Bible anymore when it was so handily on your phone? Plus, then I could act like I was paying attention, but really sneak a peek at social media every once in a while. It wasn't like I hadn't heard this sermon fifteen times over the course of the week.

I sighed.

How had I ended up here? The pastor's wife?

Would I have married him if he'd told me up front he wanted to be a pastor?

Maybe.

Probably not.

The clock at the top of my screen notified me he'd only been preaching five minutes. This would be a long service. I glanced to my right to find no less than ten people looking at me. I smiled and acted like I was highlighting sections in my virtual Bible, occasionally looking up at my husband adoringly.

Five minutes down, four million to go.

"You look lovely today, Clara," one of the older attendants commented as she did every Sunday. It didn't matter that I wore a new outfit every week, or that I spackled my face in gallons of makeup, or that my naturally blonde hair was teased within an inch of its life and secured on top of my head. I could have worn a paper sack, and she would have told me I look lovely.

Anything to get in good with the pastor's wife.

"Thank you," I said as she turned to my husband to complain about the new layout of the church seats. This week it was the seat layout. Next week it would be the carpet. Nothing would ever be perfect enough. I didn't even want to imagine what she really thought of me.

"Have you read that new book by Elena VanMoss?" Judy—the wife of board member, Vern—asked, her bony fingers on my shoulder.

The book she was talking about was the one on how to

be more like Jesus and less like Satan. Was she trying to tell me something?

"I haven't gotten around to it," I said. "But it's on my to be read pile."

As if.

If I were going to read seven hundred pages, it would be the newest Stephen King novel.

"Miss Clara!" A tiny little boy came running up to me. "Are you leading kids church on Wednesday?"

"Yep." I smiled. "As long as you promise to be there."

"I promise." He giggled and bounced away.

I knew he would be there. He was always there. His family was one of the anytime-the-church-doors-are-open sorts.

"You got the lesson plan for the children's program, right?" Judy asked. Her copper hair streaked with grey and permed within an inch of its life framed her slightly wrinkled face.

"I did," I said.

"And no making adjustments this month. We wouldn't want to confuse the kids." She didn't wait for my answer before walking away toward her husband who looked about as thrilled at her approach as I had been.

Last month I changed the lesson plans a tiny bit, and I'd been thoroughly tongue-lashed for it. I would not make that mistake again.

Even though Devon was technically head of the church —the board being primarily a financial advisory board— the men on the board were not only big wigs in the church, they were big wigs in the community.

Vern—and consequently, Judy—being the biggest wigs.

Vern had been the head football coach for the high school team the last time they'd won the state championship years ago. And Judy was chair of various philanthropic groups. If we ostracized the board, our church would go down the toilet.

"Right, honey?" Devon said.

He was speaking to a group of women who acted like my friends at church but snubbed me when they saw me in the grocery store.

I smiled sweetly. "Of course, Dear." That was my go-to answer.

"Awesome," one of them said.

"I can't wait," another said.

I looked at Devon questioningly, but he had moved onto another conversation.

With *Sydney*.

The worship leader.

She batted her eyelashes and giggled uncontrollably every time she was around him. She had the voice of an angel and a face to match. But she was at least ten years younger than we were—in her early twenties. The only reason the board gave her the position was because of how she looked.

Well, okay, and because she could sing.

"Did you like worship today?" she asked, always seeking his approval.

"It was wonderful," Devon said. "I think the Holy Spirit really works through your voice."

She giggled.

Again.

I slipped my hand into Devon's. "I thought it was good too." My voice was tense.

Her smile froze. "Cool." She paused. "I should probably go talk to the band." She gave Devon one last smile and walked away.

"I'm going to talk to the guys for a minute," Devon said, kissing me on the forehead before walking toward his group of friends—the ones he hung out with outside of church functions.

"Ugh, was that Sydney?" Lisa asked waddling over, her pregnant belly making it impossible to zip up her winter coat.

"Yep. My favorite person," I said. *"Oh Devon, did you like my songs?"* I made my voice higher and ditzier.

Lisa looked around and frowned at me. "You really shouldn't mock her with so many people around."

"What does it matter?" I asked. "No one sees me unless I'm with Devon. I could wear all the makeup and jewelry in the world, and I'd still be invisible without him."

"Don't say that," she said. "If it weren't for you, everything would be a mess. You are the heart of this church."

"Only because I have to be. It's in the pastor's wife contract."

"Oh yes, the contract," Lisa said in a mocking tone.

I laughed. "You know what I mean."

"And so do you," she said. "You might not want to do all the things you do, and you may feel unnoticed, but the church would fall to shambles if you didn't."

"You have to say that because you're my best friend," I said but was thankful for her support.

"Ooh," she grunted, her hand pressing into her stomach. "Here, feel this." She grabbed my hand and placed it where hers had been. A tiny foot pushed beneath her skin.

I choked back my emotions so they didn't come spilling down my cheeks again.

"It's the best part of being pregnant," she said. "I can't wait until you have a little one of your own."

I couldn't either.

"Do you think we could get together and watch *Love in Reality* together tomorrow?" I asked.

Even before Blake—the third in our friend group—had helped produce the show and unwittingly became a guest star, we were fans. But since Blake and Lisa had kids, our viewing parties had become sparse.

"I'll see what I can do," Lisa said, not making eye contact.

That was a no.

"Did I hear you say you watch *Love in Reality?*" Judy said from behind me.

I turned and smiled. "You did," I said. "Do you watch the show too?"

"Oh, heavens no." She looked disgusted. "It's of the devil, you know." The volume of her voice rose slowly. "I don't see why a pastor's wife would ever watch such filth."

"Pastor Devon might never have come to our tiny mountain town if it hadn't been for that show," Lisa said, her mother hen coming out. "Well, the show and Clara."

Judy scoffed. "He wasn't a pastor back then."

She was right. He wasn't. If he had been, I never would have dated him. "The show really isn't that bad."

"It's practically *pornography*," she shouted the last word. If people hadn't been listening before, now every head in the foyer turned toward us, including Devon's. His friends covered their laughs with their hands.

"I wouldn't call it pornography," I said, trying to keep my voice calm.

Her hands shook by her sides. "It is obvious you need prayer."

"Don't we all?" I kept my tone light even though my teeth clenched.

Judy didn't respond. She just stood and stared at me.

Every breath in the foyer was held. No one had the nerve to talk back to Judy. No one with a brain, anyway.

"Okay, okay." Devon's voice finally rose above the room. "I hope you all have a wonderful week. Let's get home before the roads get any worse than they already are."

Never once had he needed to kick people out of the church.

Until now.

I held in a sigh and tried to smile as we spoke to almost everyone before they exited the building.

Big Mountain was a small tourist town in the heart of the Colorado Rockies that sparkled in the winter. Between the snow and twinkly Christmas lights, it was breathtakingly beautiful.

But the beauty was lost on me today as we drove home.

"What happened back there?" Devon asked.

I crossed my arms over my chest. "Judy said I shouldn't be watching *Love in Reality* because it's pornography."

Devon just stared ahead.

"You've talked about how you were on the show," I said. "That we met on set."

"Yes, but you weren't a pastor's wife at that point. I wasn't a pastor, though they portrayed me as the saint."

"The *virgin* saint," I corrected. He'd been so handsome. So innocent. Perfect for my own innocent heart.

He was something of a celebrity after the show, but even with all the attention, he only had eyes for me.

At first, we'd been on fire for God. A team. Serving the world. Our hearts joined for one purpose.

When had that stopped?

Oh, right. When he announced he wanted to be a pastor, after I'd already said, "I do." Now, we lived in a fishbowl, and even my TV habits were under a microscope.

"Do you think I shouldn't be watching that show?"

"I'm not going to tell you what your convictions should be." The tone of his voice told me exactly what he thought my convictions should be. "But you probably shouldn't talk about it so much in church."

I sighed and looked out the window, twirling my wedding ring around my finger.

Another thing I needed to change about myself. I'd add it to the list.

"What did you think of my sermon today?" Devon asked, changing the subject.

"It was fine." Had he forgotten I'd listened to him tweak it every single day this past week?

"Fine?" Panic flooded his voice. "What do you mean, fine?"

"I mean it was good, great. Perfect."

"Do you think I messed up the second section?"

I wracked my brain to figure out which section he was talking about. His weekly sermons blended together in my mind. "No. I think it was all really good." I gave him the most convincing smile I could muster.

He glanced at me out of the corner of his eye then returned his gaze to the icy roads. Snow fell in large flakes making the entire landscape shimmer in the partial sunlight of mid-afternoon.

"How's Lisa doing with this pregnancy?" Devon asked.

"Same as all the others," I said. "Everything is documented and in order. She'll have this baby with near military precision all while managing a household, social engagements, and her husband's schedule."

Devon smiled. "She's tough."

"The toughest woman I know." And she definitely was. Always making sure everything and everyone was in order while keeping that beautiful smile on her face. "Maybe we could think about trying for a baby sometime soon?"

The question hung in the air, and for a moment, I wondered if I'd asked it aloud.

Then Devon drew in a deep breath. "I think we should wait a while longer."

This had been his answer every time I'd brought it up since we'd been married. After our wedding, we'd gone on mission trip after mission trip, only coming home long enough to see our friends and family before hopping on another plane. Obviously, that hadn't been the best time to have a baby. We were young and had all the time in the world to settle down, to build our life.

But now we were back in the states.

"Why a while longer?" I tried to keep my tone light. I knew I needed to tiptoe carefully around this subject.

Devon squeezed the steering wheel so hard his knuckles turned white. "There's just a lot going on right now with the church, and our apartment is way too small to add another person."

"Our lease is almost up. We could get something bigger," I said. I tried to keep my heart detached from the subject because, if I thought about it too long, I'd get weepy.

"We can't afford something bigger right now, Clara."

"Then I'll get a job." I was begging now. "I have a degree."

"The church needs you. I need you. And if we have a baby, it will need you."

I choked back tears and dropped the subject. I'd ask again in another year.

Walking into our apartment made me want to scream. The longer we lived there, the more it felt like the walls were closing in on us. Even if I didn't get a job, we had enough money in the bank to pay for a bigger apartment. But Devon hated spending money on things he felt were non-essential.

I kicked my shoes off on the mat—thankful for the relief—and headed to the bedroom to change into my favorite hoodie and yoga pants. As I unbuttoned my blouse, I noticed Devon staring at me.

I smiled. It had been a long time since he'd looked at me as I undressed. Maybe he was rethinking his stance on babies.

"Why are you taking off your clothes?" His tone was not sexy.

My heart sank.

"I'm getting comfortable." I reached up and pulled my long blonde hair from its headache-inducing topknot. "I do this every Sunday when we get home from church."

"We have people coming over this afternoon, remember? The board members?"

It took every bit of my willpower not to throw myself on the bed, crawl under the covers, and refuse to come out.

So much for a day of *rest*.

I reluctantly buttoned my shirt and pulled up my knee-length ruffled skirt. My hair was just going to have to stay down. I couldn't imagine putting it back up with the throbbing pain growing in my head.

"What would you like me to make for lunch?" I asked, trying not to let my frustration show.

"Anything is fine. Maybe tacos?"

At least tacos were easy.

"Don't you have your women's Bible study tonight too?" Devon asked.

I'd completely forgotten.

"Did you forget?"

I couldn't admit that I had. He'd tasked me with trying to create community among the women of the church.

Anxiety that had been building for months crept up my chest. I'd had the book for weeks, but hadn't brought myself to open it. I would have to read at least the first chapter and create talking points. All after I played hostess to the board members. Wasn't staying at the church to speak to every last parishioner enough for one Sunday?

"Earth to Clara?" Devon waved a hand in front of my face. "You forgot, didn't you?"

I looked down at my hands, trying to steady my breathing.

"It was in the announcements. And several of the women talked about it after service."

That was the conversation I came into too late. If only I'd been listening. I rarely had to. Most of them only wanted to talk to Devon, not me.

"Do I need to cancel it, or are you going to be able to get it together?" His tone was full of disappointment.

"Get it together? Are you serious?"

"Yes, I'm serious." He paused. "I'm over here working day and night to build this church. And sure, you listen to my sermons every week. But do you think I don't notice you playing games on your phone during service?"

I could feel the heat rising in my cheeks. "I don't—"

"Don't even try to defend yourself. I'm not stupid, Clara."

I closed my mouth and gritted my teeth. If you can't say anything nice, keep your mouth shut, my mother always said. All the not nice things were begging to be released if I just parted my lips.

"Don't you care about my dream? Being a pastor is all I ever wanted."

That was it. I couldn't stay silent any longer.

"No. It isn't all you've ever wanted." Words spewed from my mouth like a broken dam. There was no stopping the flow. "You *never* told me about this dream until you were offered this position. *Never*. I had no idea I would have to be this perfect little pastor's wife. That we'd live in a teeny tiny apartment. That we wouldn't have kids."

"I want kids," Devon said through gritted teeth. "Just not at this very moment."

"Then when?" I threw my arms in the air. "When we're not busy every waking second of the day? When we don't have luncheons or hospital visits or prayer times or worship practice? We're not even on the worship team."

"I'm the head of the church. A brand new church. I have to be part of all of it."

"I know you do, but why do I? It's not my job. I don't get paid. I wasn't made to be a pastor's wife. I wasn't made to smile so much my face hurt. I wasn't made to lead a Bible study full of women who know more about the Bible than I do."

"God can mold you into who he wants you to be."

"Mold me?" I was practically yelling now, but I didn't care. "What's wrong with me?"

"You're the most stubborn person I know. You can only have it your way."

"Trust me. This is not *my way*." I waved my arms around. "I never expected my life to be like . . . like this."

"Well, I'm *so* sorry you're disappointed with *God's* plan."

The condescension in his voice sent my anger through the roof. Every part of me wanted to tell him to make his own stupid tacos.

"I need to go to the store," I whispered. "Anything else you need for the board members?"

Devon didn't reply.

I yanked my car keys from the hook and slammed the door behind me.

CHAPTER 2

*D*ivorce.

It was one of those words that when it got stuck in your head, it was like a sticky burr, it wasn't coming free without taking something with it.

As I drove through the slush to the local grocery store, divorce was all I could think about.

Christians don't get divorces.

Pastors don't get divorces.

It would ruin his *dream* if we divorced.

But what about my dreams? Had he stopped to consider those? I was a stay-at-home mom with no kids—a stay-at-home pastor's wife. Expectations were heaped on my back as if I were some sort of camel.

I mindlessly walked through the grocery store, grabbing everything I'd need to make the tacos—something I'd perfected in my college days. My mind flashed to Lisa and Blake. They were living their best lives.

Lisa was second on my speed dial list. I tapped her name on my screen.

"Hello?" her voice was tired.

"Hey, Lisa," I said. I could hear her two-year-old screaming in the background as usual.

"What's up?" Lisa asked, her voice slightly impatient.

"I can't do this anymore." I fought back tears as I added ground beef to my cart.

"Can't do what anymore? Jacob, don't stand on the back of the couch, you'll break your head open."

I ignored the chaos and tried to continue with the conversation. "I can't be a pastor's wife. I'm just not cut out for it. It's all a big mist—"

"Jacob," her stern voice interrupted. "If you don't get off that couch in two seconds, you will sit in timeout, mister." She sighed. "Sorry, Clara. What were you saying?"

"It's just that I'm not pastor's wife material. *You* should have been the pastor's wife. You're the perfect person to be a pastor's wife." I pictured her perfectly clean, perfectly decorated house.

Lisa laughed. "I'd be a terrible pastor's wife. I'm too blunt. People would hate me. Okay, Jacob, it's timeout time." She groaned. "Sorry, Clara. Can I call you back? Everything is crazy around here right now."

"Sure," I said, but the phone had already disconnected.

I tossed two packets of taco seasoning into the cart and wiped the tears from my eyes. Maybe Blake would have time to chat. Just as I was about to hit her name on my speed dial, a voice from my past came from behind me.

"Clara, is that you?"

I turned to find the only man who had ever broken my heart standing in the taco aisle.

"Hi, Brian," I said, trying to smile.

"Are you okay?" He closed the gap between us and pulled me in for a hug like it hadn't been ten years since we'd seen one another. He smelled like cinnamon gum and mangos.

"I'm fine. It's just been a rough day," I said as he released me. "How have you been?"

"I've been good," he said, his smile as white as the snow falling from the sky. "Busy in New York."

I looked down at my shoes. How could something still sting after so long?

"What are you doing in town?"

"I'm consulting for the hospital," he said. "Plus, I haven't been home for Christmas since . . ."

Since he'd broken my heart and moved halfway across the country. "I'm sure your parents will be thrilled to have you home," I said. "And if you'd like, you're welcome to visit our church."

"That's right, you married a pastor," he said. "How's that going?" His voice held a hint of laughter. If anyone knew how wrong it was for me to be a pastor's wife, it was Brian.

"It's going really well," I lied. "The church numbers are growing faster than we can keep up."

He stared into my eyes, searching me like he always did. "But how are *you*?"

Everything in me wanted to break down and cry on his shoulder, tell him how awful it was. But that would be entirely inappropriate for a married woman, let alone a pastor's wife. Devon probably had multiple text messages already that Brian and I were talking in the grocery store. Gotta love small towns.

"I'm doing well. Really. Everything is a bit crazy with Christmas coming up, but once we get into the New Year, life will slow back down." I glanced down at my watch. I needed to get home so I could get the tacos together before the board members showed up. "I don't mean to cut this short, but I have to get going."

"It was nice seeing you." He wrapped his arms around me for one last hug.

I let myself sink in for the slightest moment then backed up. "It was nice seeing you too."

"In order to continue to grow, we will need to expand the church building," Holden, one of the younger board members, said to the group of men as I handed them plates of tacos.

My mind was back at the grocery store. Cinnamon and mango still filled my nose.

"I don't know that we need to add onto the church. We have empty seats every Sunday," Vern said.

Brian had aged everywhere but his eyes. They looked wiser. Every other part of him looked as youthful as the day he'd walked away from me. Did he think I looked older?

"But what happens when we don't have empty seats?" Holden asked. "It won't be long before the entire community is coming to our church."

The night we'd broken up flashed in my mind.

"We can't think like that," Devon cut in. "We're not here to steal people from their home churches. We're here to bring in people who have never stepped foot in a church."

He'd taken back his promise ring and boarded a plane to New York for med school.

Silence overtook the dining room for a moment as I cleaned the kitchen, remembering all the tears I'd cried.

"Regardless of how they're getting to us," one of the board members finally said, "we'll need a place to put them every Sunday."

Devon had been my rebound.

"What if we add another service?" Devon said.

My mind screeched to a halt at Devon's words.

Had he said *another* service? Sundays would be twice as long? Would I have to go to *both*?

"The church was only built two years ago," Devon continued. "Adding on now might not be the best option."

"I think two services, or even three, could make a difference," Vern said.

Three? I scrubbed the counter more vigorously, all thoughts of Brian pushed to the back burner.

"As long as it doesn't make it look like no one's coming to church," Vern continued. "Empty seats stir up fear in parishioners. They think there's something better out there."

"We'll fill them," Devon assured him. "Even if it means going door-to-door again, we'll get people in those seats."

I could have cried. Door-to-door was my least favorite task.

And I always had to go.

"Just take Clara with you," one of the guys whispered. "She'll get them to come."

A couple of the men laughed. What was so funny about that? Was I so entertaining that people came to church to watch me suffer?

"Yes, take her. As long as she doesn't speak about the demonic shows she's been watching," Vern said. "I think you need to talk to her about that. Judy is very upset about the incident today."

"I've spoken with her," Devon said.

"And will she stop watching?" Vern pushed.

"She is her own person. I have advised her to do what she believes God would want her to do. Everyone has different convictions."

Was he actually standing up for me?

"If she continues to watch that program, things may have to change at the church," Vern warned.

Devon didn't answer right away. "I'll talk with her again," he finally said.

No.

He was not going to tell me what I could and couldn't watch in the privacy of my own home.

"Then it's settled," Vern said, his voice returning to normal. "We'll advertise a second service, go door-to-door, and save the money we would have spent on an addition."

The meeting came to a close shortly thereafter.

"I'll go to the church this evening so you have the house

to yourself for the women's group," Devon said before heading to the gym that afternoon.

I grunted in acknowledgment. We hadn't discussed the extra service, the door-to-door invites, or *Love in Reality*. He knew I'd heard their conversation, but he didn't seem to care.

I fumed as I finished cleaning the apartment. My Bible and the Bible study book were buried under a pile of blankets and clothes in our bedroom.

Judy had suggested the book to Devon, who then forced it on me. She had already read it and would be coming to the group. She should have been the one leading the study, but Devon had insisted it be me.

By the time the first woman showed up—Judy, of course—I was at least partially prepared. Not only had I read the first chapter, I had gone online and gotten some cliff notes to make sure I knew what to discuss.

"That skirt must be so comfortable," Judy said.

"Why do you say that?" I looked down at the ruffled skirt I'd put on that morning.

"You've worn it all day. I have such a hard time finding comfortable skirts. Where did you get it?"

Was she being nice to me?

"It's from the Gap," I said. "I've had it for a while, but they might still carry it."

"I've never shopped at the Gap before. I might have to try it sometime." She leaned in a little closer even though we were the only two people in the apartment. "Though I wouldn't wear it to the pastor's wives retreat if I were you. It might come off as too—" She waved a hand in the air "—modern."

23

As if modern was a bad thing.

She helped herself to the decaf coffee I'd set up neatly with creamers, sugar, and little stir sticks on my kitchen counter. "How do you like the study? Have you gotten a lot out of it?"

There was only one right answer to this question. "I have enjoyed it very much."

"Good." She stirred in the tiniest bit of sugar. "When I saw it at the bookstore, it screamed your name."

I glanced at the cover of the book. It had a picture of a wilted flower and the words *Restored by God* as the title.

Is that how they pictured me? A tired, wilted flower in need of restoration?

She sipped her coffee and winced. "This coffee is bitter. I guess I'll have to break my diet and add cream."

"It's the newest local roast. I thought we could try it."

She patted me on the arm, her eyes filled with mock-sympathy. "Maybe you should stick with what the board has decided is the best coffee for the church."

By the board, she meant her. Coffee-gate had been one of the first issues we'd come across as a new church. But, wouldn't you know, Judy came out on top.

"I thought since this wasn't really a church function—"

"This most definitely *is* a church function," she said. "Even though we're holding the group in your apartment, it's still a church-funded and church-sanctioned group." Her voice had turned to pure nastiness. "Next time, use the *right* coffee."

I mumbled an okay.

"Have you reconsidered watching that awful show?" Her tone was threatening.

What was she going to do? Fire me as pastor's wife?

Then dread filled me, what if she somehow got Devon fired because of this stupid show? If anyone had the power, Judy did. And as much as I hated my role, I didn't want Devon to lose his dream.

"I guess I'll stop," I lied.

What she didn't know wouldn't hurt her. It wasn't like she knew where I was every moment of every day. And Lisa and Blake would never tell—if they ever watched with me, that is.

Speaking of, Lisa and Blake took that moment to enter.

"Hey ladies," I said, sidestepping what I suspected was a follow-up question from Judy. "I'm so glad you could make it." I hugged each of them.

Judy looked Blake up and down, starting with her frizzy black hair and nose ring all the way to her torn jeans and combat boots. She made punk look effortless and almost classy.

"Don't say anything about *Love in Reality*," I whispered to them when Judy wasn't listening.

"Sorry about this afternoon," Lisa said. "Are you doing better?"

"I'm fine," I said as convincingly as I could. "Just a bad day."

She and Blake smiled. She'd probably filled Blake in on their way over.

By the time we began, women filled my entire living room. So much so it was almost impossible not to be touching someone else.

"I'm so thankful all of you came tonight," I said. "I know it's a tight fit, but what better way to draw closer to one another and God at the same time."

Blake and Lisa smiled in support. Judy crossed her arms in front of her. Sydney looked around as if surveying the place.

"Everyone has a copy of the book, right?"

Nods from all around the room.

"And who read the first chapter?"

Every hand rose.

"Fantastic." I opened my book. "Let's start at the beginning with the questions the author asks."

Someone cleared their throat.

"The first question was—"

The throat cleared again.

I glanced up to find the offender.

Judy stared straight at me with her hand in the air.

"You don't have to raise your hand. We're all free to discuss openly." I smiled.

Judy looked affronted. "Where's the civility in that?"

I held my tongue.

She continued, "You forgot to pray for the group."

Ah, yes. Indeed, I had. "Thank you, Judy," I said, bowing my head. "Heavenly Father, You are so good. You rescue us when we need You. You open doors for us to walk through. You give us strength when we are weak. Please give us wisdom as we walk with You through the study. In Jesus' name I pray, amen."

I looked to Judy for her permission to continue, but she was whispering something to Sydney.

"Now that we've prayed, let's start with the questions. Would someone like to read the first one?"

The study went relatively well overall. Judy only inter-rupted ten or twelve more times to interject the way she would have managed the group. I nodded and went along with her ideas. I'd caused enough drama for one day.

"Shall we end with prayer?" I asked.

"I think we should do a prayer and praise report," Judy said, not bothering to raise her hand anymore.

So much for civility.

Prayer and praise reports were a slippery slope. They usually started out harmless—helpful even—but could end up being total gossip fests.

"I think that's a great idea," I said. "However, let's leave out specific names. If you'd like us to pray for some-one, just give us the circumstances—not too detailed, though. God knows who they are. We don't have to."

Some of the women nodded, others looked like I'd just dumped cold water down their shirts.

There were more praise and prayer reports than I had expected, and we prayed for a solid hour. My back ached from sitting cross-legged on the floor for so long.

"If there are no more prayers?" Most of the women looked just as tired as I was.

"I have one more," Judy said. She had offered up most of the prayer reports only thinly veiling whom she was talking about. "I'd like to pray for someone in our congre-gation I worry about daily. She seems distant from God, and her ability to be close to God is of utmost importance to the church's well-being."

Was I being paranoid, or was she praying for me?

I looked up, and she was staring me down like a hawk locked in on its prey.

"This woman doesn't think the church is as important as her own life and should do more to help her husband and the rest of the congregation. I am also worried about her taste in clothing, the skirts she wears are much too modern."

The other women shifted in their seats. Blake let out a little gasp. And Lisa looked like she might have hit Judy if they weren't on opposite sides of the room.

"Would you like me to pray, or would you like to?" I asked, playing dumb.

"Why don't you pray for this *woman*?" Judy said.

I bowed my head and folded my hands. "God, please watch over the woman Judy is describing. Help her know what she needs to do to please You above all else. Give her the fashion sense that would best represent You, God. Amen."

When I looked up, Judy was still glaring at me.

I took the opportunity to dismiss the group. "Thank you all for coming."

I'd been in groups where we stayed and talked for hours afterward.

This was not that group.

Everyone left within minutes. Blake, Lisa, and I exchanged hugs before they let themselves out.

When the door clicked into place behind them, I took

off my offensively modern skirt and pulled on the yoga pants that had been begging me to wear them all day.

"You must have had a great group tonight," Devon said, walking through the front door. "I've been waiting in the car so I didn't interrupt."

I didn't respond. I was exhausted. My brain was fuzzy. And all I wanted to do was climb into bed and stay there for the next month.

"So?" Devon asked.

"So what?"

"How did it go?" His tone was pushy, and it sent flames of anger into my cheeks.

"It went fine."

"Fine?"

"Yes fine. We did the study. We prayed. Judy made me feel like a child and criticized the clothes I wear. It went fine." I sat on the edge of the bed.

"You know, you could learn a lot from Judy. Many people look up to her in the church."

"Like *Sydney*?" I said.

"Yes, like Sydney, and many others."

"I won't ever like her. She's awful," I said, folding my arms across my chest.

"That's unfortunate because she's been assigned to do the door-to-doors with you next week as we ramp up for Christmas services."

He hadn't even asked. It was as if I was his puppet.

"I'm not going door-to-door. Judy can go herself."

"The board specifically requested you, and I think it would be good for you."

"Do you think it will *restore* me? Make me that perfect pastor's wife?"

He threw his hands in the air. "It couldn't hurt."

My mouth fell open. Three words confirmed what I'd feared he thought about me.

I didn't have any fight left inside me.

"I need some air," I whispered, taking the car keys.

I left before I said what was on my mind.

That one terrible word.

Divorce.

My head begged for it. It would be so easy. We didn't have children or pets or even plants. Our belongings were so minimal it would take five minutes to determine who got what.

I pulled out onto the icy road, my back tires slipping a bit. I let off the gas and corrected the motion. Snow swirled around the back of a semi in front of me, causing a temporary whiteout.

I should have gone home and dealt with Devon. But my pride wouldn't allow it. How dare he tell me I'm not a good enough pastor's wife? Even if I wasn't, it wasn't like I didn't try. Like I hadn't given up everything to go along with him on this adventure.

I darted out around the semi to see if anyone was coming from the other direction.

No lights.

Taking the opportunity, I hit the gas to pass.

My mind reeled. Where was my life heading? How had I become this bitter person? I'd been so happy in high school. College even.

"Where are You, God? Why have You put me here?" I

yelled in the privacy of my car. "Give me a sign. Tell me what to do!"

A horn from the semi jerked me to attention, but it was too late. The elk hit my hood and came right through my windshield.

I slammed on the brakes, but my car lost what little traction it had. The last thing I remember was rolling once and then twice.

CHAPTER 3

"*C*lara?" A man's voice came from somewhere distant, echoing through my head. "Oh no, Clara!" The voice grew louder and more familiar.

I tried to talk, but the words wouldn't leave my mouth. My eyes were sealed shut. I couldn't move my limbs.

"Doctor, do you know this woman?" a woman's voice whispered.

The world spun. I felt like everything was moving too fast. I was going to vomit.

"Yes. She's my—uh—a friend." It was the same voice I'd heard at the grocery store earlier.

Brian.

"What happened to her?" he asked.

Footsteps moved all around me, almost in unison. We were moving.

"She was in a roll-over accident," the woman said. "Lucky to be alive. The semi she was trying to pass stopped, and the driver helped. He wrestled the elk out of her car."

"Elk?" Brian asked.

"She hit an elk. It went through the windshield. He said it was struggling to get free."

"Bull or cow?" he asked.

"Cow. If it had been a bull, he would have killed her with his antlers."

I tried to open my eyes again and failed.

"The minute she wakes up, please page me," Brian said.

"I will," another woman's voice said. This one was older and gentler than the first.

His footsteps faded.

"What could have made you want to pass a semi in this weather?" she whispered.

The argument flooded back into my mind. Devon's words cut just as deeply as they had when he'd said them.

I needed to get out of this marriage. I needed a second chance at happiness.

"Can you hear me?" the nurse asked. "Squeeze my fingers if you can hear me."

Her soft cool hand rested inside my grasp. I tried to squeeze. Was I squeezing?

"Good. Good girl," she said. "Can you open your eyes?"

If I could squeeze my hand, I could open my eyes.

The lights were so bright they sent pain through my body like volts of electricity.

"Sorry, sweetie," she said. "Let me turn the lights down."

The lights dimmed, and I tried again, successful this time.

33

She picked up a phone on the wall and whispered a few words into the receiver before turning back to me.

"Do you know what happened?"

I started to nod but stopped.

This was it—my answer.

I didn't have to remember. I didn't have to remember anything.

If I didn't remember, Devon and I could part ways, and he could keep his job.

"Do you know your name?" she asked.

"Clara Henderson." My voice came out sounding like a toad's.

"Yes, your name is Clara." Her sweet face looked down at me. "But your last name is Langley."

I did my best to look confused.

"And what is the date, Clara?"

The date? What was the date?

"December something?"

"Okay," she said slowly. "And do you know where you live?"

"In an apartment on Aspen Drive with Blake and Lisa." Before I'd ever met Devon.

She glanced at her chart, which likely had my current address.

"You're awake," Brian said, walking into the room, a grin on his face a mile wide.

"I thought you moved to New York." I tried to make my tone as irritated as I could. I'd forgiven him years ago, but if I was going to make this believable, I had to sell it.

"I did," he said, glancing at the nurse.

"I asked her a series of questions," the nurse whispered, pointing to something on her clipboard.

Brian's face paled in recognition.

"Clara." Devon ran into the room. "Oh my goodness, Clara." Devon scooped me up in his arms.

It was now or never.

I stiffened. "Who are you?"

"I'm your husband." Devon gently lowered me back to the bed.

"I'm sorry, but I'm not married."

Devon looked back and forth between Brian and me.

"What's going on?" Devon asked, wiping tears from his eyes. "What are *you* doing here?"

"I'm consulting with the hospital for a few weeks." Brian took a step toward Devon. "It looks like Clara has some retrograde amnesia."

"Only temporarily, though, right?" Devon asked.

"We can't know at this point."

They both glanced down at me. I wanted to stand up. Be eye to eye at least. But my body was sore in so many places and still didn't want to move.

"What's the last thing you remember?" Devon asked me.

"I remember Brian telling me he was moving to New York. That I was holding him back."

"You met me not long after that," Devon said. "On *Love in Reality*."

"I was on *Love in Reality*?"

"No. I was," Devon said. "As one of the contestants, not as the lead. That was Katarina."

"I remember her. And Shane was on the show, right?"

Shane was Blake's ex-boyfriend and her husband's brother. It was a long story.

Devon nodded eagerly as if my memory was coming back. "And you and I met on set at a concert."

I looked down at the white sheets in front of me. "I'm sorry. I don't remember that part." I glanced up at him. "I wish I did, though. You're very handsome."

The nurse let out a little laugh. Brian huffed.

"You will remember. I know you will. God has all of this in His hands."

Brian rolled his eyes behind Devon.

Devon sat in the chair next to me but didn't grab my hand.

Tears stung at my eyes. How could I put him through this? But then his words echoed in my head. He didn't think I was a good enough pastor's wife. After everything I'd done to try to be what he needed.

This would be for the best. We could get divorced. He could stay pastor. And marry someone more fit to be his wife. The thought took away what little breath I had, but it was the only way.

"I'm tired and confused," I said. "I know you want to stay . . . I'm sorry, what was your name?"

"Devon. My name is Devon."

"Devon." I nodded as if this were new information. "I know you think staying will help, but I'm in a great deal of physical pain, and I think I need rest."

My husband looked stunned. "Can I pray for you before I leave?"

"Pray for me?" I asked. How would a younger Clara have answered? "I suppose that's okay."

He moved to take my hand but retracted and instead laid his hands in his lap. "God, I know You have all the answers. Please help Clara remember our life together. Heal her body and her mind. Though I know she would be well received in Heaven, I am thankful she is still on Earth with us. In Your precious name, amen."

I opened my eyes, trying to keep the tears from falling. "Thank you."

Brian sighed.

"I'll be back first thing tomorrow morning," Devon said. "If anything changes, please call me."

"Of course," Brian said, walking Devon out.

The nurse stared at me.

"What?" I asked.

"You, my dear, are one lucky lady to have those two men fawning over you."

"Even if one dumped me because I was too small town and the other is a stranger?"

"Even so," she smiled.

"I'm in so much pain," I said. "What is wrong with me besides my head?"

"You were scraped up pretty badly," she said. "You have stitches in several places. But you came out with only minor bumps and bruises."

Minor? I could feel them.

All of them.

It was like my entire body was one big bruise. "How long will I be in here?"

"I'll have to check with the doctor," she said. "But for now, you should get some rest."

My eyes were only closed a few seconds before I was off in dreamland.

"Clara?" Lisa's motherly voice popped into my dreams.

I opened my eyes to a blast of early morning sunshine, and Lisa and Blake and a huge pot of daisies.

"Hey," I said with a small wave.

Lisa wore leggings with heeled boots and a tight white long-sleeved t-shirt that accentuated her growing belly. Her Auburn hair was pulled back into a tight chignon, and her makeup was flawless. No matter how hard I tried, I'd never been able to do my makeup as beautifully as Lisa did hers.

"Oh wow," I said in my most surprised voice. "You're pregnant?"

Lisa glanced at Blake, who looked equally beautiful in her leather jacket, torn jeans, and curly black hair cascading over her shoulders.

"Devon told us you were having a hard time remembering," Blake said.

"Devon?" I asked. "My husband?"

Blake set the vase in the windowsill and leaned against the wall. Lisa carefully lowered herself into a chair.

"How are you feeling?" Lisa asked.

"I'm better now," I said. "They gave me medicine for the pain."

"You hit an elk," Blake said. "A gigantic cow elk."

"The accident was terrible," Lisa said. "God was really watching over you."

I felt instantly guilty. I hadn't thanked God for saving my life. I could have easily died.

Thank you, God. Thank you so much.

"Do the doctors know when you'll get out of here?" Lisa asked.

I shook my head.

"Where are you going to live?" Blake looked at Lisa. "We don't have the apartment anymore."

I hadn't considered that. Think back. My parents.

"I'll live with my parents," I said.

"Your parents moved to Florida," Lisa said.

"They moved?" I asked. "Did they sell our house?"

They had, and I had been devastated. I'd come back from a mission trip, and a huge sold sign stood on the front lawn.

"It's okay," Lisa said, trying to calm me. "Just breathe."

I took a deep breath and steadied my voice. I still couldn't think about my parents selling that house without choking up. "I'm sure the two of you have built lives for yourself."

They nodded.

"What's the last thing you remember?" Lisa asked.

"Brian leaving," I said.

"And after that?" Blake said. "Do you remember the season *of Love in Reality* at Big Mountain Lodge and Resort?"

"I remember part of it. Shane being on it, that jerk."

Blake laughed. "It was for the best. I ended up with his brother."

"Dan?" I acted surprised.

Blake nodded.

"He was the one I meant to set you up with in the first place," I said.

Blake smiled. "And I'm eternally grateful."

"You met Devon on *Love in Reality*," Lisa said. "He was one of the contestants. The virgin."

"He mentioned something about that last night," I said.

"I'm sure this is a lot to take in," Lisa said. "Do you want us to stop?"

"No," I said. "I want to hear about everything." I took a sip from the hospital-issued water jug. "Are you married too?" I asked Lisa.

"You probably remember Jesse and the accident."

I nodded. Her high school boyfriend had died in a serious accident. She still didn't like to drive in the snow. Thank goodness I hadn't died the same way.

"After that, I had a hard time dating until Dan introduced me to someone."

"Do you have more kids?" I asked. It was a tiny bit scary how easy it was for me to pretend I didn't know all this.

"I have one other," Lisa said. "A little boy named Jacob. This one is a girl." She rubbed her stomach.

"And do you have any, Blake?" I asked.

"Dan's daughter was a teenager when we got married," she said. "Then we had the twins a few years later. They're the same age as Lisa's Jacob."

"You were pregnant together?" I asked.

I was on a mission trip for their pregnancies. When I returned to Big Mountain, they each had their little bundles of joy. It was the first time of many when I felt left out in their presence.

"They're best friends now." Lisa smiled. "The three musketeers."

"But I don't have children, do I?" It was a question I would have asked, but it was physically painful for me to ask it.

Neither of my friends answered right away.

"I think you want children," Lisa said. "But when you and Devon married, you went on multiple mission trips. Then he was in seminary. And now you're building a church."

"Oh," I said.

"But there's still time," Blake said. "I'm sure you'll have a whole flock of little ones soon."

Little did they know, I'd probably never have children of my own. Especially since I was about to divorce my husband.

"How's my favorite patient?" Brian asked as he walked into the room, his eyes widening at the sight of my friends.

He looked fresh—his brown hair soft and feathery, his face clean-shaven. I'd always had a thing for the metro-sexual guys—the ones who dressed as well, if not better than I did. The ones with a chiseled jawline that could have been models, but instead became doctors. Or pastors.

"Hi, Blake." Brian cleared his throat. "Lisa."

"You're her doctor?" Blake spat the words from her mouth as if they were live crickets.

"I am," Brian said.

"I thought you were in New York," Lisa said.

"I'm in town for a while consulting for the hospital," Brian said, looking through my chart.

"And then you'll be leaving again?" Blake asked.

"That's the plan." He looked up at me with a hesitant smile.

Blake and Lisa glanced at me too.

I shrugged. If my friends found out what I was doing, they might never speak to me again. I'd always been the good Christian girl—the one whose morals stood out from the rest.

And now I was a liar, a fake, a fraud.

A sinner.

"I can come back later if you'd like," he said. "You look like you're doing okay."

"Not so fast." Lisa pushed up out of her chair, leading with her belly. "What do you think of this whole amnesia thing?"

Brian studied her as if trying to come up with the correct response. "I've seen several cases of it. It happens in many types of accidents."

"And do the patients typically get their memories back?" Lisa was interrogating him.

"I've seen patients get their memories back, but some don't. Ever." He looked down at his cell phone. "I need to be in surgery in twenty minutes. Maybe we can catch up another time?"

Blake scoffed.

Lisa followed him into the hall to whisper-yell at him.

"She just doesn't want to see you get hurt again.

Neither of us do." Blake sat down. "I'm sure you remember how badly he hurt you."

I nodded.

She twirled a curly hair around her fingertip. "Plus, you're married, right? I mean, even if you don't remember him, you're still married. That's gotta mean something to God."

Especially since God knew I was faking. "I don't know if I can stay married to someone I don't know."

"You could get to know him," Blake said gently. "He's a great guy. He makes you happier than Brian ever did."

Did he? All I could think about was our fight. How he thought I was less-than.

"Lisa said we were building a church," I said. "How in the world did I become a pastor's wife?"

Blake stopped twirling. "You fell in love." She smiled. "You and Devon are the sweetest couple. You'd do anything for one another. When he said he wanted to be a pastor, you jumped right on board."

I had, hadn't I? Why hadn't I dug in a little? Helped him figure out if being a pastor was what he really wanted?

"Do you still work at the resort?" I asked.

"I own it," she said.

I did my best excited-surprised expression. "You *own* it?"

She blushed. "Yeah. Dan and I bought it a few years ago from the previous owner. It's been a fantastic investment."

Especially since she'd completely revamped the place.

"The pre-Christmas women's retreat is happening next

week. You planned on being there before your accident . . ."

"I'll still come." It was one of my favorite events, after all.

She leaned over and hugged me so tightly I thought the stitches in my head might pop out. "I thought we lost you." Emotion flooded her voice, making it raspy and quiet. "Your car is completely totaled."

They'd had to drive by the accident scene to get to the hospital. I imagined how I'd feel if I'd seen either of their cars wrecked. My stomach clenched. "I'm okay," I squeaked out between my tears.

"I leave for five minutes, and you're both in tears?" Lisa said with a laugh. "That guy hasn't changed a bit." She motioned to where she had been speaking with Brian. "I don't want you getting mixed up with him. He's trouble. Has been since elementary school."

"We should probably go." Blake leaned over to hug me again. "We'll be back soon."

Lisa hugged me as best she could with her belly.

"Call if you need anything," Lisa said. "We love you."

"I love you too," I said.

Would they still love me when they found out the truth?

CHAPTER 4

*D*evon arrived not long after my friends had gone.

"Good morning," he said when he peeked his head into the room. "Do you mind if I come in?"

"Of course," I said, sitting up in my bed.

He wore the khaki pants I had gotten him for Christmas a year ago with a white button-down shirt that showed off his ridiculously toned biceps. The buttons weren't lined up with their proper holes, and his sandy blond hair was completely disheveled, making him look even sexier than usual.

"Any chance you remember me?" Devon looked at me hopefully, placing the huge vase of red roses he'd brought next to the daisies from my friends.

I shook my head.

Bags drooped under his eyes. He looked like he had aged overnight.

He sat in the chair next to my bed. "I thought maybe I

could tell you some things to try to bring back your memories?"

"Sure," I agreed. How could I say no?

"I started to tell you a bit about how we met on *Love in Reality*."

I nodded.

"The woman on the show—the lead—didn't like me at all. Probably because I was a virgin." He laughed. "You and I had an instant connection. It was fantastic. We dated for a couple of months before we got married in the church you grew up in." He smiled as if remembering that day. "It was raining so hard, the roof started to leak, and all the guests left mid-ceremony. They ended up having to rebuild not too long after that." He laughed. "Then we traveled all over the world as missionaries until God placed it on my heart to become a pastor. You were so supportive." His eyes misted a bit. "You told me to go for my dreams."

Why had I been so compliant?

"And now our church is one of the fastest-growing in the state. All because of you."

He wiped an escaped tear.

"What do you mean because of me?" I asked, expecting him to list all the things I do for him—for the church.

"Because you're there for me to lean on, even when we have hard times." He looked away.

"Were we having hard times when I got in the accident?" I tried to keep my voice neutral when I wanted to shout at him.

He stared out the window. "Yes. We had just gotten into an argument."

"About what?"

"It doesn't matter," he said. "I'd rather you remember the good, not the bad."

I wanted to push but decided against it.

"Knock knock." A voice at the door propelled him to his feet.

Sydney.

Her hair was perfect in two long French braids over her shoulders, her makeup subtle, and her dress so form-fitting it looked like she was going to a club, not a hospital. She held a bouquet of chocolate-covered fruit on sticks.

"Hi Sydney," Devon said.

She handed him the basket with a flirty smile. "How is she?"

Jealousy flared inside me. "I'm fine," I said. "And who are you?" I had no obligation to be nice to her now. It was freeing.

"I'm the worship leader at Devon's church." She batted her eyes at him when she mentioned it being *his* church.

"It's not my church," he corrected. "It's God's church."

"Of course you'd say that." She brushed a hand against his arm then turned her attention to me. "So you don't remember anything? Like, do you know the ABCs and stuff?"

"A, B, C, D, E, F, G, H, I, J, K, L, M, N, O, P, Q, R, S, T, U, V, W, X, Y, Z." I sang as out of tune as I could just to see her cringe.

"Clara's forgotten the past ten years. Retrograde amnesia," Devon explained. "But we're hopeful she'll get her memories back soon."

If there was one thing that made me want to come clean, it was seeing this woman fawning all over my husband.

God, please don't let him pick her as his new wife.

"You don't remember Devon?" she asked me.

"Nope," I said.

"Oh, Devon." She touched his arm again. "That must be so hard for you."

He walked away from her and back to my bedside. "She'll pull out of it soon, and then everything will be back to normal."

Normal. Ugh. I hated that word. I hated normal.

"Are you married, Sydney?" I asked.

Sydney blushed. "Oh no. I'm saving myself for someone special. I always thought I'd marry a pastor, though."

"Is that why you're hitting on my husband?" I asked.

Sydney's face went white.

"Not that I have any feelings about it, obviously," I continued, "since I don't remember him being my husband, but it's painfully obvious you're trying to get his attention."

Devon tensed beside me, staring at the floor.

"It's okay," I said. "Though, I don't know how God would feel about it."

"I think I'll go now," she said slowly.

Devon smiled and nodded.

"Thanks for the chocolate fruit," I said with a wave.

When she was out of the room, Devon turned to me. "Did you really just say that?"

I thought he might be mad, but when he looked at me, there was laughter on his face.

"She had it coming." I shrugged. "Did I completely hate her when we were married? I mean, I know we're still married, but . . ."

"You certainly didn't like her. But she's never been so forward with me."

Yeah. Okay. Like every single day.

"Well, I hope I didn't squash any chances you might have with her now that—"

"Don't even say it. You will get better. God will heal your mind. And even if he doesn't, I will do everything in my power to show you how much I love you so you can fall in love with me all over again."

Why couldn't he have acted this way when I didn't have amnesia? Why did it take me getting into a car accident for him to care? I sucked in a breath. I had to make him understand.

"But you're a pastor," I said.

"Yes," he said.

"I'm not like Sydney," I said. "I always said I would never marry a pastor."

He frowned. "You have? I don't remember you ever telling me that."

That's because I didn't think it was important. He went to school to be an accountant.

"Why wouldn't you want to marry a pastor?" he asked.

"I'm not exactly pastor's wife material."

"But you are a fantastic pastor's wife."

I wanted to roll my eyes. Last night he didn't think I was such a good pastor's wife.

"You head up a Bible study, you do a door-to-door outreach, and you're great with the kids."

My heart tightened. I *would* miss teaching the kids.

"It just doesn't sound like me," I said. "I'm sorry, Devon."

He looked like I'd slapped him across the face. Part of me expected him to say he'd quit, give it all up for me. But he didn't. Instead, he reached down into a bag he had sitting next to his chair legs.

"Maybe these will help," he said. "This is a picture of us on our wedding day." He handed me a picture taken from our living room wall. "And this was the first time we went up to the cabin together. You couldn't possibly forget the cabin." His voice was desperate, almost pleading. "We've been there every year since we've been married." He waited expectantly as if I might regain my memories in a flash.

"As in my parents' cabin?"

"It was our wedding gift." His voice now distant, dejected. He stared at the photo.

Was he remembering the year we'd gotten snowed in and had to pee in a pot because we couldn't get to the outhouse? Or maybe the time we'd caught fifteen trout in one afternoon, releasing them all back into the river after naming them.

It hurt to know what I was giving up, but the thought of his disappointed face last night solidified my decision. "I just don't remember. I'm sorry."

Devon grabbed the photos and lined them up on the

windowsill.

"Excuse me?" A nurse popped her head into my room.

"Yes?" I said.

She walked in a bit further. "We have plans for you to be released first thing tomorrow morning."

"Thank you," I said. I needed to figure out what I was going to do.

"I'm guessing you're not going to come home when you're released," Devon said.

I shook my head. "I can't. It would be too weird."

He stared out the window.

"I think Lisa and Blake are working on a place for me to stay."

"At least you remember them," he said. "Your parents said they'd be here just as soon as they get back from their cruise."

My parents had five kids—all boys except for me. They'd never done anything for themselves. And this year they decided to take their very first vacation, just the two of them. "I'm glad they went on a cruise."

Devon smiled. "Me too. They deserved it." He looked down at his watch. "I should probably get going. I have a lot to get worked out now that you're out of commission. That is, unless you want to head our door-to-door outreach campaign?"

"Door-to-door outreach? What is that?"

"Basically, exactly what it sounds like. You go door-to-door, talking to people about the church and inviting them to come. You're good at it. Everyone knows—knew—that if you went, we'd get a great turnout."

"It sounds excruciating." I wrinkled my nose for effect.

"It is. I'll let you off the hook for now," he said with a wink. "I'll be here tomorrow when they release you."

"You don't have to do that. I'm sure Blake or Lisa—"

"Whether you remember or not, I'm still your husband." His tone was full of more love than I'd heard in what felt like years. "I love you, Clara."

I almost replied that I loved him back. It was my automatic response. But I kept the words in. His persistence would make it hard to hold out for that divorce. But I had to. It was the best thing for both of us.

CHAPTER 5

itting in a hospital bed alone was incredibly boring. Daytime TV wasn't much help, and the romance novel one of the nurses dropped off had me blushing within ten pages.

"Who's ready to watch *Love in Reality?*" Blake popped her head into my room. The smell of pizza assaulted my nose, making me salivate on the spot.

"Oh my goodness, you're my hero," I said, my voice giddy. "Hospital food is awful."

Lisa looked just as perfect as she had that morning. "It's not all bad. The pudding is yummy."

"You just think that because you're pregnant," Blake teased.

"Don't worry, we'll all be catching up on this season since we don't have the time to get together as much anymore," Lisa said, handing me a paper plate with a slice of gooey pepperoni pizza.

At least they'd made time this week.

The show started like always with the recap from the previous week.

"Ooh, I bet everyone hates her." Blake pointed to the blonde on screen who talked like she was chewing bubble gum even when she wasn't.

Sitting with my friends, enjoying pizza and bad reality TV without a care in the world like old times made me feel better than I had in months. I'd missed this.

"What is he doing?" I asked when he picked bubble gum girl in the elimination ceremony. "He can't pick her. She's so terrible."

Both Blake and Lisa agreed, adding their own comments.

"Next week on *Love in Reality*," the host said, "we will go to a private beach resort . . ."

The TV flashed to the women in string bikinis, a couple of them blurred because they were so inappropriate.

A gasp from the doorway turned our heads.

Judy.

Her eyes were glued to the TV.

Lisa clicked it off. "Hello, Judy. It's nice of you to visit."

"I thought she wasn't going to watch that show anymore." Judy plopped her green potted plant on the table next to me. "I thought you weren't going to watch that show anymore."

"I'm sorry, Judy, I don't know if you were informed, but Clara has amnesia," Blake said her tone on the verge of condescension.

"Oh, I heard." She walked closer and got right in my face. "Is that true?" Her breath smelled like the church's

54

coffee. They must have had an emergency board meeting tonight.

"Yes," I said. "Judy, is it?"

She straightened up. "I'm one of the board member's wives."

"Our board members have multiple wives?" I asked. "I guess I never asked what kind of church we started when Devon was here."

Blake snorted. Lisa turned her head to look out the window at the dark sky.

"Of course not," Judy said flustered. "I meant I am married to one of the board members. I am his *only* wife. And as for you, I would have expected you to get your memories back by now. You seem perfectly okay."

"Just some stitches," I said. "But this darn brain of mine won't let me remember the last few years."

"So you're not going to go door-to-door with me this week?"

I shook my head.

"Not leading bible study?"

I shrugged.

"Not helping with the Wednesday night children's program."

My heart jolted.

"No," I whispered, trying to keep the tears out of my eyes and my voice.

"You're taking yourself out of the church completely?"

I suppose I was.

"She'll still *attend* church," Lisa said. "Right, Clara?"

I'd attended religiously since I was a kid. It would break character if I said no.

"Yes," I said. "I'll still attend."

"And I'll take over the Bible study," Lisa said.

Judy stared at her. She had probably wanted to take that honor. Or to give it to Sydney.

"And I can go door-to-door with you," Blake said.

We all turned and gaped at her. Other than the occasional Bible study, Blake wasn't much of a church attender.

"What?" Blake asked.

"It's just you—" Judy started, but Lisa interrupted.

"Would be perfect for the job." Lisa smiled. She was enjoying this.

"And how about I continue to work with the kids," I said. "I've done that as long as I can remember."

"That will only confuse them," Judy said. "How will they feel when you can't remember their names?"

"Children are surprisingly understanding," Lisa said, her tone non-negotiable. "Now that we've taken care of all that, what else can we do for you, Judy?"

"I came to see if there's anything I can do to help," Judy said. "But that awful television smut distracted me."

"I don't know that there's anything you can do to help," I said. "My memories will either come back, or they won't."

"Devon isn't taking this well, you know," she said. "He's very distracted, which is not good for the church. If he can't get it together—"

"Then what?" I asked. "Are you going to fire him? Because he's going through a family emergency?"

She looked taken aback.

"That seems pretty un-Christian-like, don't you

think?" I continued. "Would Jesus have put someone on the streets, taken away their livelihood, because they were having a few bad days?"

Drawing herself up and smoothing the front of her tailored pantsuit, she said, "Of course I'm not threatening his job. I have no such power. I just want you to know how much better everything would be if you got your memories back."

"Point taken. I'll try to heal just as fast as I possibly can," I deadpanned. "And thank you for coming to visit."

She took the hint and left.

Both Lisa and Blake stood open-mouthed, staring at me.

"What?" I asked.

"No one challenges Judy like that," Lisa said. "Not even me."

I shrugged. "Is she so important she can treat people like dirt?"

"Yes. Yes, she is," Lisa said.

"I can't wait to go door-to-door with her," Blake said.

"Don't get too excited," Lisa said. "She'll put a kibosh on all expansion plans until Devon is back to himself."

Blake deflated a bit. "I would have loved to talk her ear off while she stared at my nose ring." She reached up and touched the tiny diamond stud in the side of her nose.

"I forgot to tell you," Lisa said. "Mrs. Wilton insists that you stay with her. Both Blake and I would take you in, but she's getting older, and I think she'd like the help around the house."

Mrs. Wilton had been our next-door neighbor when we'd lived in the apartment where Blake's stepdaughter,

Hannah, now lived. She had been a grandmother, a counselor, and a shoulder to cry on through college.

"I would love to stay with Mrs. Wilton," I said.

"We'll be back in the morning with Devon to get you out of here," Lisa said as she tidied the room. "He's gathered your things together so you'll feel right at home."

"And we'll help with your hair and makeup, so you look perfect when you leave this place," Blake said, squeezing my hand.

"Thank you. You are the best friends a girl could ask for," I said. "And maybe once I'm out of here, I'll be able to get a job. I mean, I don't think it's right of me to spend Devon's money since I don't remember being married to him."

"That's both of your money," Lisa said.

I wanted to object. The last time I'd made an actual income was when I was a barista in college. Never once had I used my degree in library science.

But all that would change. This was my fresh start.

My second chance.

CHAPTER 6

*I*n the dead of the night, I went for it. I was jonesin for a fix. My mind needed it. My eyes needed it. My fingers needed it.

I opened the bag with my possessions. My wedding ring glistened from one plastic corner. I hadn't even noticed it was missing from my hand.

I pushed away the guilt and went for what I'd initially set out to get—my phone. The screen lit up when I powered it on. Immediately I went to my social media to find dozens of get-well messages and comments.

Then the dinging started.

It was like my phone might actually blow up. I switched the vibrate button on, but it was too late.

"Is everything okay in here?" Brian poked his head in the door.

I considered shoving the phone under my blankets, but that would look more suspicious than it already did.

"I—I was just . . ."

Recognition spread over his face. I was caught.

"Okay, don't hate me."

"Why would I hate you for not understanding how to use today's technology?" Brian sat in the chair next to my bed. "Can I help you?" He held out a hand for my phone.

I handed it to him with a sigh of relief.

"Good job getting it turned on," he said. His hazel eyes were warm and caring. So different from the night everything ended. Maybe Lisa was wrong. Maybe he had changed.

"This is a touch screen phone. There are no buttons like the old phones."

I nodded as he explained how to open apps, how to text people—it was unlimited now—and how to make a phone call.

"Have you been happy in New York?" I asked quietly, interrupting his speech on closing out of apps to save the battery.

"I have," he said. "Medical school in New York was amazing. I will always love that city. And I was engaged to a model—an actual model."

This stung a bit. It wasn't like I was ugly, but I was nowhere near model-pretty.

"Sorry, that came out wrong," he said, noticing my reaction.

"So you're married?" I looked down at his finger—no ring.

He shook his head. "Things didn't work out. She got spooked, and I haven't seen her since." He gazed into my eyes. "Plus, I think I always compared her to you."

"Me?" I asked.

He rubbed the back of his neck. "Yeah. You've been the

standard for the women I've dated. I thought my feelings for you had changed, that I'd grown up and moved on, but then I saw you in the grocery store."

"The grocery store?"

"Yesterday. You looked like you had been crying. And when I hugged you, it was like time hadn't passed at all. Like it was fate bringing us back together."

"You broke my heart," I said.

"I know," he said. "And if I could take it back, I would. If only a few additional months would have been erased from your memory."

I wanted to be angry with him. If he'd been saying this to me mere weeks after we'd broken up, I would have been. But I wasn't. It was so long ago. And he was here now, telling me how much he missed me.

"I'm married," I said stupidly.

Why was I defending the marriage I was so eager to get out of?

"But you don't remember being married."

I shook my head.

"Where does that leave us?" he asked.

Us? There was an us now?

"I don't know," I said. "This is all so confusing."

Did I want him back? Never once had I imagined I'd find someone else if Devon and I divorced. It was never about that. But it wasn't necessarily out of the question.

"I'd love to have a second chance with you." His words hung in the air like a dense fog.

This wasn't supposed to be so complicated.

61

"Are you ready for your makeover?" Blake announced at the door as she, Devon, and Lisa walked in the next morning. Blake held up makeup boxes, and Lisa waved around a brush and curling iron.

"It's not like I'm going to prom," I said. "I'm just being released from the hospital."

"You really don't have any memory," Blake said. "That's the old Clara talking."

"Is the—uh—new Clara high maintenance?" I asked.

No one answered for a minute.

"I wouldn't say high maintenance," Devon said gently. "More like keeping up with expectations."

"Whose expectations?" I asked.

He shrugged.

Lisa and Blake both had confused looks on their faces.

"At some point, you just decided you needed to look the part," Devon said. "Whether someone said something to you, or you just did it, I'm not sure."

I wracked my brain. Surely someone had told me what was expected of a pastor's wife. It was probably one of the mentors at seminary. Or Judy.

"I'm okay if you don't make me look like a Barbie," I said. "Maybe just some jeans and a hoodie?"

Forty minutes later, I felt more myself than I had in years—jeans and a hoodie, hair down and straight, and makeup barely there. It reminded me of all the times in high school the three of us had sat around doing each other's hair and makeup, talking about boys. Except this time, we didn't talk about boys much, especially since one of them was in the room with us.

"You look wonderful," Devon said. "I've always liked you better with less makeup."

He did? Why didn't I know that?

"I think I have everything packed up in the car," he said. All the flowers and cards that had been on windowsills and tabletops were gone.

"I've been meaning to give this to you." I pulled my wedding band from the plastic bag. "I think you should hold on to it."

He looked down at the piece of metal that hadn't left my finger since the moment we said, 'I do.'

"Okay, sure." He plucked it from my palm. "I'll hold on to it for now."

Time felt like it had slowed. Neither of us moved.

"Everyone ready?" Blake asked, popping into the room.

"Yep." I smiled at Devon.

He returned the smile with a fake one of his own.

Mrs. Wilton looked frailer than I'd ever seen her. When Blake, Lisa, Devon, and I walked into her apartment, she didn't get up to greet us but waved from the couch. Her hair and makeup, however, were on point, as always.

I sat next to her, and she wrapped an arm around my shoulders. "You look beautiful, dear."

"Thank you," I said. "So do you."

"Probably a lot different from how you remember me." Even her voice was frail.

"Yes," I admitted. She hated it when we lied to make her feel better. She always urged us to be honest with her.

"Where should I put her things?" Devon asked. He had packed up what seemed like my entire closet in several suitcases.

"I'll show you." Blake lead him into one of the two unused rooms.

Mrs. Wilton's apartment was a mirror image of the one Blake, Lisa, and I had lived in next door except decorated with a whimsical old Hollywood vibe.

"Can I get either of you anything?" Lisa asked us.

"You? Get us something?" Mrs. Wilton laughed. "You look like you're ready to explode, my dear. Please sit down. You're making me tired just looking at you."

Lisa smiled and lowered herself into an armchair. "Are you feeling well?" Lisa asked Mrs. Wilton.

"I feel like an old woman. But I'll be less lonely with Clara's company." She turned to me. "I'm happy to have you here. God works in mysterious ways, and you are an answer to my prayers."

Would God use me while I was chest deep in sin sludge?

"And you're an answer to mine," I replied.

"You're all set up," Blake said when she and Devon walked out. "Is there anything else you need before we leave?"

I shook my head. "Thank you so much for everything."

Blake helped Lisa out of the chair and they both hugged me.

"Let us know if you need anything, okay?" Blake said. "And Hannah is right next door. Feel free to call her too."

Hannah was finishing her degree in elementary education. Her mother died during childbirth, and her father raised her by himself until he and Blake got together. Blake adopted Hannah as soon as humanly possible, and they all lived happily ever after. Well, for the most part.

"You can also call me if you need anything," Devon said, standing awkwardly in front of me as if he didn't know if he could hug me. "I'd like to see you every now and then if you're up for it. If your memories aren't going to come back, I'd like the opportunity to win your heart again."

"I think that's acceptable," I said.

"And I'll see you tomorrow night for children's church, right?" he asked.

Lisa must have informed him about her conversation with Judy.

"I'll be there." I smiled. "Is there a lesson plan or anything?" My mind flashed to Judy reminding me not to go off the lesson plan.

"There is," he said, leaning in a bit, "but I'd like to see what you can do without it. Your memory loss might have the benefit of giving you some free rein to do things the way you would like. I think our church could use a bit of revamping in the children's program." He straightened up. "But don't tell Judy I said that."

We all laughed. If Judy knew he was blatantly going against her plans, she'd call for his head.

"Can I hug you?" Devon asked.

"Sure," I said.

His hug felt like home. It wasn't awkward like it should have been. Like *I* should have been.

He pulled back and looked into my eyes. "I know you won't say it back, but I love you, Clara."

I smiled.

"We'll see you soon, okay?" Lisa said. She and Blake hugged me again before filing out of Mrs. Wilton's apartment.

I sat down next to Mrs. Wilton. "Is there anything I can get you?"

"You can get me a big heaping plate of the truth," Mrs. Wilton's said, her frail voice replaced with the one I knew so well. The one that was strong and fierce.

"What?" I asked.

"I know you've made up this amnesia complex." Mrs. Wilton was never one to tiptoe around the elephant in the room. "Out with it. What has gotten into you?"

"Nothing," I said. "I don't—"

"If you lie to me one more time, young lady, I'll kick you out of my house. You'll be homeless. Stubborn and homeless."

Well. not quite. I *could* go live with my friends.

I sighed. "How did you know?"

"I was an actress. You—I'm sorry to say—are not."

"Everyone else is buying it."

"Are you sure?"

I shrugged. "Are you going to tell them?"

"If I was going to tell them, I would have already."

"Why didn't you?"

"It's not my story to tell. Not my monkey, not my drama." She leaned forward and took my hand in hers. "What's going on? Why have you gone to such extremes? Is Devon hurting you?"

I shook my head. "No. Of course not."

"Then what?" she said. "Because this is not something a sane person would do."

"It seemed right in the moment." I looked down at our hands. Hers old and wrinkled, mine still smooth but starting to show age. "I want a divorce. But if I had asked for one, it would have crushed Devon. And he'd have been kicked out as lead pastor. You can't be a divorced pastor."

"It's a shame that's the way churches operate."

Mrs. Wilton was more of a spiritual person, less of a religious person. I didn't quite know where she stood on the whole believing in Jesus thing, but I loved her just the same.

"It's a hard position for churches to be in," I said. "On one hand, you want to be loving and accepting of everyone like Jesus was. But on the other, you need someone in a leadership role who walks the walk and talks the talk. How would Devon, as a divorced pastor, council newlyweds? Or those having marital difficulties?"

"I see your point," she said. "But I still don't like that it's put you in a position where you've practically lost your ever-loving mind. Why do you want a divorce, anyway? Devon loves you. You've always seemed so happy together."

"We are," I said. "As a couple—when the church isn't looming over us—we're great. That trip we went on a couple of years ago to the Bahamas felt like a second honeymoon. We were us again."

"You're placing a lot of power in the church."

"I guess it's not so much the church, but the expectations the church—and Devon—have of me. I'm expected to be perfect. To carry the weight of the world on my shoulders. To do whatever I'm told with a happy heart. It's exhausting. I just can't do it anymore."

"Crazy idea, but stay with me," she said. "What if . . . you talked to Devon about this?" She enunciated her words slowly and carefully as if she were speaking to a child.

I wanted to roll my eyes, but I knew Mrs. Wilton wouldn't take kindly to my disrespect. "I've tried. He doesn't hear me. In fact, he thinks I need to be an even *better* pastor's wife."

Mrs. Wilton patted my hands and sat back. "Well then, I'm right here with you. We'll get you that divorce if that's what you really want."

"Really?" I asked. "You'll help me?"

"You make a convincing case." She shrugged. "But I think you should tell Blake and Lisa. They *are* your best friends."

"It's bad enough I've made you an accessory to my sin."

"Accessory to your sin?" She let out a barking laugh. "That's one I've never heard before."

"I don't feel like they should have to lie for me. Nor should you."

"Eh, God's all-forgiving. He'll get over it," she said. That's the way she lived her life, after all. "Now tell me, what's the plan? Are you going to forget forever? Or will you eventually come back to your senses after the divorce is final?"

I had no idea.

"You didn't plan that far out, did you?"

"No. It was sort of a spur-of-the-moment decision." I

thought for a moment. "The first thing I need to do is get a job."

"A job," she said. "That'll be easy. Where do you want to work?"

"My degree is in library science," I said. "Do you know if the local bookstore or library is hiring?"

"I know everyone in this town. If I tell them to hire you, they will."

I laughed but knew she wasn't joking. I'd have a job by the end of the week.

hen I arrived at the church on Wednesday evening, Devon greeted me warmly at the door. "I was worried you wouldn't come."

"After sitting in Mrs. Wilton's apartment all day, I was happy to get out for a bit."

"The kids are excited to see you." He led me down to the children's section of the church. It was my favorite with bright colors, the smell of crayons and stale goldfish, and lots and lots of laughter.

"Miss Clara!" Emma screamed over the commotion. She darted at me and tackled my legs. The other kids followed.

"Okay, okay. Be careful with Miss Clara," Devon said. "She's still not all better."

"Do you remember my name?" Emma asked.

"Let me guess," I said. "Fiona?"

She shook her head, giggling.

"Tiffany?"

She laughed louder.

"Haley?"

"Emma," she said, not able to take the guessing game anymore.

"Emma, of course! You look just like an Emma," I said. "Maybe we should make name tags so I can learn your names again."

"Can mine be pink?" Emma asked.

"Absolutely," I said.

The other kids started chiming in with all the ways they'd decorate their name tags.

"You good?" Devon asked.

"Perfect," I said.

"If you need any help, just call." He slapped his forehead. "Sorry, do you even know how to work your phone?"

"Brian showed me," I said before I could stop myself.

Devon's smile fell. "Good. Well, I'll just be going then."

He left, and I only had three seconds to feel bad before the kids regained my attention.

Once we'd gotten the craft supplies from the closet, we began making our name tags.

"Did you know God has a whole bunch of names?" I asked the kids.

"Like Jesus," Emma shouted.

"Very good, Emma," I said.

"But God can't have lots of names," one of the boys said. "That's too confusing."

"What is your mommy's name?" I asked.

"Jenny," he said.

"But what do you call her?" I asked.

"Mommy," he said.

"Already, your mommy has two names. Isn't that cool?" I asked.

He smiled. "Yeah. And my daddy calls her Sweet Sugar Love."

I did my best not to laugh. Kids were so brutally honest, and I loved it. "That's a lovely name."

"I think it's gross," he said.

"Did you know that in Proverbs it says the name of the Lord is a strong fortress?" I asked.

"What's a fortress?" A girl around four asked.

"A fortress is like a castle with walls all around it, protected from all the bad things," I explained. "And after it says the name of the Lord is a strong fortress, it says the godly run to him and are safe. So if you run to God and call him by name, you will be safe."

Some of the kids smiled, others were so focused on creating their name tags. They probably didn't hear me at all. Either way, it felt nice to be here, teaching the kids without expectation.

After the children had been claimed by their parents, many of whom wanted to know everything about my accident and offered condolences and any help I needed, I grabbed my coat and headed for the door.

Mrs. Wilton had allowed me to use her car since mine was beyond repair, and she didn't drive anymore. As I was about to walk outside, I realized it would be terrible of me not to say goodbye to Devon.

He was probably in his office practicing his sermon for the weekend.

"Do you need anything? Anything at all?" A voice I couldn't stand was coming from Devon's open door. "I could bring you dinners or—"

"Thanks, Sydney, but I'm okay," Devon said. "I know how to take care of myself."

"But you shouldn't have to," Sydney said. "You have more important things to think about than making meals."

"It's a good thing there's a diner just down the road," he said. His voice seemed tired. More tired than usual. "But thank you. I appreciate your kindness."

"Anytime. You can call me day or night." She turned and walked right into me. "Oh, I'm sor—" she stopped and took in my face "—oh, it's you."

"Yep, just me," I said. "Still trying to hook a married man?"

"I'm trying to be like Jesus. Feed the hungry and all," she said in a melodic tone.

"Okay," I said sarcastically and then turned to Devon. "I just wanted to tell you I was leaving."

"Can I walk you out?" he asked.

Sydney huffed and walked away.

"Sure," I said.

"Hang on a second. I have something for you." He pulled a gift bag from behind his desk. "It's nothing big, but I thought you could use some of your favorite things while you're away from home."

He handed it to me, and I peeked inside. Pizza flavored Pringles, a lavender-scented candle, the new

73

Steven King book, peppermint gum, and a bag of my favorite coffee.

"You might not remember that these are your favorites but—"

"It's perfect," I said. "Thank you." He wasn't joking when he said he would try to win back my love.

"How was it tonight?" he asked. "Were the kids well behaved?"

"They were wonderful." I told him about the name tags and how we talked about God's different names.

"I knew you'd do great," he said. "Will you come back again?"

"It would be my pleasure." I stopped at the door before walking out into the cold winter air. "Why don't we have kids?" I asked, looking up into his face.

He twisted his wedding ring around his finger. "I don't know."

"Do we want kids?" I asked.

"Yes," he said slowly.

"But we haven't had any?"

"It's complicated. We have been so busy with everything." He stopped twirling his ring. "I guess that's not a great excuse."

"Is there more to it than just being busy?" I tried to keep my tone neutral. This wasn't my life. This was a life I wasn't supposed to remember.

He shrugged. "It's scary, you know?"

I smiled but said nothing. Sometimes silence was best.

"It's hard making ends meet on a pastor's salary with just the two of us. Kids are expensive." He seemed to be talking more to himself than to me at this point. "I mean, we have quite a bit of money saved. But it's not enough. What about college? And sports? And diapers? It's just so much." He dropped his shoulders. "And I don't think I'd be a very good dad."

My heart fell to my feet. "What do you mean you don't think you'd be a very good dad?" He'd never told me this before.

"Let's just say my father wasn't exactly the best of role-models."

That was putting it lightly. His father had gone to jail for domestic violence when Devon was ten. He'd almost killed Devon's mother and left Devon with a broken arm.

"But you're nothing like that," I said without thinking.

Devon glanced up at me.

"I mean, you seem like a great guy is all."

"They say those things pass from generation to generation—violence." Tears glistened in his eyes. "They say boys who are abused will become abusers."

I reached out and rubbed his arm. "I've only known you for a couple of days, but even I can see you're not an abuser."

Devon wiped the tear from his eyes. I wanted with every part of me to hug him until he felt better. To tell him how he would be an amazing father. If only he'd told me this when I had my memory.

"Thank you for your kind words," he said with a smile. "I don't know why I told you all that."

"Had you told me those things before?" I asked.

He shook his head. "No. I don't know that I could have verbalized it before."

Devon held the door open for me, the blustery air rushing toward my face.

"Thanks for your help tonight," he said. "For what it's worth, I'm sorry we don't have kids."

I turned away before he could see the tears in my eyes.

CHAPTER 8

*T*he smell of paper and ink surrounded me. I was in heaven.

As promised, Mrs. Wilton had gotten me a job at a bookstore. Technically, she'd gotten me a job at the bookstore *and* the library. But working in the children's section of the bookstore sounded better than re-shelving books.

At least for now.

"I'm so happy to have the help," Elaine—the owner—said. "I've never had children and don't relate particularly well to them. It would be wonderful if we could enhance that department."

"I'll do what I can," I said. "Where would you like me to begin?"

"Could you start with the Christmas decorations? I don't seem to have the time or energy to get this place looking festive."

"Sounds fun," I said. Christmas was my favorite holiday, and I loved decorating. "Where are your decorations?"

"They're up in the attic, at the top of the stairs take a left. There's a doorway that leads to another set of stairs into the attic."

"I'm on it," I said. It was a good thing I wore comfortable shoes and had taken my pain killers that morning. My injuries were healing nicely, but I was still pretty sore.

The attic was like most attics: dusty and packed full of stuff. But Elaine kept it tidy and organized. Finding the Christmas decorations took less than five minutes. Carting them downstairs, however, took the better part of an hour.

I started on the tops of the bookshelves, adding garland and lights, then worked my way to the stairs, weaving lights around the banister up to the loft.

As I was finishing upstairs, the bell rang, indicating someone had entered the shop. I peeked downstairs to find Judy removing her hat and gloves.

I ducked down so she couldn't see me.

"Judy, it's so nice to see you," Elaine said.

"And you," Judy said. "I got the message that my books had come in."

"Ah, yes." Elaine pulled a stack of books from behind the counter.

"Can you please put them in a paper bag?" Judy asked, her tone frantic as she glanced around to make sure no one could see what she was purchasing.

Elaine did so quickly, and Judy relaxed a bit. "Thank you."

"I hear there's been some shakeup at the church," Elaine whispered, glancing up at the loft. The acoustics were perfect for me to hear what she said.

"The pastor's wife lost her memory. At least that's what she claims," Judy said.

I wanted to storm down the stairs and give her a piece of my mind.

"Clara, right?" Elaine said. "I just hired her today."

"You hired her?" Judy glanced, around trying to find me.

"Don't worry. She's up in the attic."

"Why would you hire her? Her place is in the church."

"Wanda Wilton asked me for a favor."

There was silence for a moment, then Judy said, "If I have to take my business elsewhere, I will."

"Where are you going to go? I know you hate ordering things online," Elaine said.

"I can't risk her knowing what I'm getting. You know how sensitive that subject is."

"I've never broken your confidentiality. Not once. And I don't plan to now."

Judy hesitated. "Fine. But if I find out—"

"I lock my records in my office. No one will see them."

Judy seemed to accept this and said her goodbyes before leaving the store.

My heart raced. What was Judy up to? What kind of books had she purchased?

"It's tradition to place mistletoe somewhere within the store," Elaine said when I walked back downstairs. "You put it wherever you like, just make sure it's up."

"Sounds good," I said, trying to keep my voice normal. As if I hadn't just overheard her conversation.

The mistletoe was in the fanciest box I'd ever seen for a fake plant. It was silver with maroon trim and weighed close to five pounds. The mistletoe was in pristine condition. I glanced around the store. The loft might be a fun place, but that might encourage full-on makeout sessions. So maybe not.

I wandered around a bit, getting a feel for the store, trying to get my mind off Judy. I hadn't been inside since I was in college, and at that point, I'd only come in to pick up my textbooks. That was before Elaine bought it and turned it into a warm and cozy atmosphere.

The back corner featured travel books, but not your ordinary travel books with the glossy photos that needed updating every year. These travel books were worn and used. Books people had taken with them and consulted on their adventures then brought back for another person to use.

I pulled one from the shelf and opened it carefully to find a photo of the Eiffel Tower and notes in French in the margins. I'd traveled out of the country many times, but never to Paris. I re-shelved the book and decided the travel section was the perfect place to put the mistletoe.

As I climbed the stepladder, I imagined a man and a woman who had never met before—something rather unlikely in Big Mountain—standing in this section looking for the key to their next adventure. They would reach for the same book and laugh as their hands touched.

"Are you going to Paris?" he would say.

"Maybe someday," she would say.

They would look up to find the mistletoe—unassuming, yet powerful—above their heads. They'd laugh a bit before she shrugged.

He would carefully take her head in his hands and kiss

her so gently she would wonder if it had even happened at all. They'd pull back from one another and smile.

"Can I buy you a cup of coffee?" he would ask.

She would simply nod as he had stolen her breath with the kiss.

I smiled.

"What are you smiling about over here in the corner?" Brian's voice startled me so badly I almost fell off the stepladder. "Whoa there." He took my arm and helped me down. "Mistletoe, huh?"

I stepped away carefully so as not to be caught underneath. Just the thought of kissing Brian made me anxious.

"The store looks great," he said. "Did you do all this?"

I glanced around at the lights and the garland and nodded.

"I'm impressed."

"Why are you here?" I asked, finally able to find my voice.

"I thought I'd bring you lunch on your first day of work." He held up a bag from the local sub shop. "Grilled peanut butter and jelly, right?"

I hadn't had a grilled peanut butter and jelly sandwich in years.

"Thanks," I said with a smile. "But how did you know I work here?"

"Word travels fast in a small town." He winked. "Should we sit?"

"Let me just make sure I'm allowed to take a lunch," I said.

"You are," Elaine said from the counter. "And he's right, this place looks amazing."

I laughed. "Thank you."

We sat in a couple of oversized chairs near the front window. Outside, the weather was blustery and cold. Snow swirled in tiny tornadoes before releasing and fluttering down to the ground.

The bookshop was a part of the town square where an enormous town Christmas tree stood proudly in the middle. Every year a live nativity brought tourists and locals together in the park.

"How are you feeling?" Brian asked.

I touched the cut on my head that hurt the most. "Still a bit sore, but nothing too bad."

"And the amnesia?"

"Still there."

His face widened with his smile. "Would you like to go on a date with me this weekend? I have Saturday night off and—"

"I don't know," I interrupted.

"I know I hurt you, and the words I said are much fresher for you, with losing your memory and all. But I want to make it up to you."

"How about being my friend?" I asked. "I'm technically married. And even though I don't remember it, I don't want to do something that would displease God."

Hypocrite. I winced. I was a total hypocrite.

"Okay then, how about you hang out with me Saturday night? As friends?"

Wasn't that basically the same thing?

"Let me think about it, okay?"

"Sure." He gave a curt nod. "I've waited this long. But

in the meantime, can I at least bring you lunch from time to time?"

"A girl's gotta eat, right?" I said.

The bell above the door chimed. Brian and I glanced over to find Devon brushing snow from his jacket. I almost jumped up as if caught doing something I wasn't supposed to.

But I was only having lunch. In a public place. With an old friend.

"Devon, hi," I said, trying to act casual.

"Looks like we both had the same idea," he held up a deli bag matching the one Brian had carried in, though I was sure his contained a turkey and cheese sandwich—my current favorite.

"You brought me lunch too?" I asked. "Did Mrs. Wilton tell you I was here?"

"Lisa did," Devon said. Bits of white snowflakes rested atop the gelled peaks of his hair.

"You can join us," I said. Brian gaped at me, but I ignored him.

"I don't know that that's the best idea." Devon hesitated.

"I'll leave," Brian stood and said. "The two of you probably have things to discuss anyway."

I didn't want Brian to leave, but I didn't want to hurt Devon's feelings either.

"I'll see you around," Brian said before walking out the door. His aloof nature had always frustrated me.

"I'm sorry. I didn't mean to kick him out," Devon said, still standing.

"You didn't," I said. "It's okay, really, sit down."

Devon took off his heavy wool coat and sat where Brian had been. "How are you feeling?"

"Sore, but mostly the same," I said. "No memories."

Devon's reaction was the exact opposite of Brian's. He deflated in the chair. "I keep praying God will open your eyes. Unlock that part of your brain that has completely forgotten me."

"Can I ask you a question?" I asked.

"Anything," he said.

"Why do you want me to get better? From what my friends have told me, we weren't in a good place when I got into this accident." Okay, so my friends hadn't told me that, but he'd likely not corroborate the story.

He looked into my eyes. "We were having a rough go, it's true. With all the stress of the church and Christmas coming up, I was in poor form." He looked around to see that we were alone. Elaine had made herself scarce when Devon walked in. "Honestly, I feel a great deal of responsibility for you losing your memory. If we hadn't gotten in an argument and I hadn't said what I had, you wouldn't have gotten in the car. You wouldn't have driven in the storm. You'd still remember me."

"What did you say?" I asked.

He hesitated. "I said you weren't a great pastor's wife."

The vulnerability in his voice made me almost feel bad for him.

"But I never should have said that."

"I thought you said I was a great pastor's wife," I said. "Or was that a lie?"

His silence cut deeper than his words had.

"I see," I said, trying to hide my emotion. "I could have guessed I wouldn't have been very good at it. I mean, I'm not exactly the type of person to be in that role."

He twisted his ring again. "It's not that you weren't good at it. Everyone loves you. It's just I could tell you didn't like it. Your heart wasn't in it."

"If you knew I didn't like it, why did you make me keep doing it?"

"Because I needed you—I need you," he said. "Since you've been gone, the church has come to a grinding halt. No one knows what to do. Including me."

"So, you want me to remember so I can make everything better for the church?" He was not helping his case.

"Honestly? Yes. And no. I mean, I'd love for things to be easier at the church, but maybe this is a blessing in disguise. It's not ideal that a church relies so heavily on one person. Your absence gives people who may have never served the opportunity.

"But more than that," he continued. "I miss you. I miss talking to you every day. I miss seeing you every morning. And it breaks my heart to know I could lose you permanently."

I didn't know what to say. If he was being honest, that meant that our life could change. That if I regained my memory, I could still relinquish some of my responsibilities.

"Did Brian ask you on a date?"

The change of subject nearly gave me whiplash.

"Yes."

"And?"

"I told him it would be wrong to date him since I'm married."

"Do you *want* to go on a date with him?" Devon asked.

Did I? My head spun. Brian wasn't even remotely my type anymore. Sure, Devon had been my rebound after Brian and I had broken up, but so much had changed. And yet, part of me wanted to know what it would feel like to see him again. Guilt settled in my chest at that thought.

Not only was I a liar, I was now an adulterer.

"If you want to, you can," Devon said. "Not that you need my permission. But perhaps spending time with him would remind you of the past. Would bring back your memories."

I could feel my jaw drop. Was my husband—my *pastor* husband—permitting me to date another man? Red flags went up in my mind.

"Are you giving me permission because there's someone you want to date too?"

Devon's eyes widened. "No. Not at all," he said. "You're my wife. When I married you, I said in sickness and health. Forever. There is no one in the world I would want beside you."

"Not even Sydney?" I looked down at the sandwich I hadn't eaten.

"Not even Sydney," he said. "I don't know where this is going. I don't know if we will end up together or—" he stopped before finishing the sentence. "But I know I will do nothing that might jeopardize our future. And that includes dating Sydney or any other woman."

I smiled. "I bet women are coming out of the woodwork to get to you now that I'm out of the picture."

He blushed. "It's a bit insane, actually."

We both laughed a little.

"Go out with Brian, if that's what you want, but give me a fair shot too, okay?"

"Deal," I said.

"How about I make you dinner tonight at our apartment?"

"I'd like that," I said.

He smiled. "Do you want me to leave this sandwich here for you?" He looked down at the sandwich he was holding and the uneaten one in my lap. "It's turkey and cheese."

"Turkey and cheese, huh?" I shrugged. "Sure, I could try it." Secretly, I was salivating thinking of the sandwich in the bag. Not that grilled peanut butter and jelly wasn't good. It just wasn't exactly my cup of tea anymore.

"I'll pick you up at Mrs. Wilton's tonight around six," he said. "No need to dress up."

"Okay. And thank you for bringing me lunch."

"I'd bring you lunch every day of the year if it would bring you back to me."

But that was the thing. He'd work to get me back, but once I was his, would he push me to the side again?

A burst of cold air swirled through the shop when he walked out the door.

"Two hunks? What more could a girl ask for?" Elaine laughed, emerging from the back office.

Clarity. I could ask for clarity.

CHAPTER 9

*M*rs. Wilton was like a Chihuahua greeting me at the door.

"How was your day?"

"Did Elaine already call you?"

"Perhaps." She smirked. "How was lunch?"

"Eventful." I hung my jacket on the old-fashioned coat tree. "Devon gave me permission to date Brian."

She gasped. "He didn't."

"Yep. And I'm having dinner with him tonight."

"Dinner with Brian?"

"Dinner with Devon," I corrected. "I haven't made plans with Brian yet. It still just seems so strange."

"Doesn't dinner with Devon defeat the purpose of your entire plan?"

"I couldn't say no. He was being so sweet and apologetic. But I think I will approach the idea of divorce tonight. I need to get the ball rolling." Even though my heart wasn't completely behind it, how could I divorce the man I had loved for ten years?

Mrs. Wilton didn't respond.

"How was your day?" I asked.

"My daughter—Nelly—called me."

"What? Wow. It's been a really long time, hasn't it?"

"Several years," she said. "She's coming to town next week and wants to see me."

"Is she bringing her daughter?"

Mrs. Wilton's eyes misted over as she nodded.

"That's wonderful," I said. "Do you need me to stay with Lisa or Blake while she's here? I could probably even go up to the cabin."

"Goodness no. You are as much a daughter to me as she is. Maybe more so."

It was my turn to get emotional. "Can I make you some dinner before Devon comes to pick me up?" I asked.

"That would be wonderful," she said, laying her head back against the couch cushion.

"Are you feeling okay?"

"It's been a busy day for this old lady," she said. "I'll be fine after a good meal and some rest."

After serving dinner and subsequently tidying up, I changed my clothes into one of my favorite pair of black slacks and a dark pink silk top that tied on the side. I left my hair down and applied a few extra coats of mascara but didn't go through my whole makeup routine.

"You look pretty stunning to be going to dinner with your soon-to-be ex-husband." Mrs. Wilton said when I emerged from the room.

I second-guessed my outfit choice. "Do you think I should change?"

"Are you going to ask for a divorce?"

"Probably. Maybe," I said. "I don't know."

She laughed but didn't answer my question.

"Will you be in bed before I get back?" I asked.

"I'll probably watch a few programs before heading that way."

I bent down and kissed her on the forehead. "Don't stay up too late."

"Stay out as late as you want," she said with a wink. "I love you."

She'd never said that to me before. I mean, I knew she loved me—she loved all of us—but she'd never actually said the words.

I stopped and met her eye. "I love you too, Mrs. Wilton."

Devon stood in the lobby with a bouquet of red roses and an enormous smile on his face. "You look stunning," he said as he gave me a small side hug and handed me the flowers. "If you'd like, I can run these upstairs."

At that moment, Hannah came through the doors. She was dressed casually in jeans and a hoodie and seemed to glide on air.

"Hey, Clara," Hannah said. "Devon."

"Hi, Hannah," I said.

"I'm surprised you recognize me," she said. "Since I probably looked different a few years ago."

"Not that different," I said, trying to cover my gaffe. "Plus, I knew you lived here."

"Those are beautiful flowers. Did you get them for her, Devon?"

I could remember a time when Hannah was so shy she would hardly talk to a guy. She had certainly grown into an outgoing young woman. Blake had a lot to do with that.

And Blake hadn't wanted kids. I chuckled inside.

"Would you mind taking them up to your apartment?" I asked. "Mrs. Wilton may already be asleep on the couch, and I'd hate to wake her. I'll come by tonight or tomorrow and pick them up."

"Sure," she said. "Good choice, Devon. These are gorg."

"Thanks," he said then turned to me.

"Hey, do you guys think you'd be up for being in the live nativity?" Hannah asked. She was the volunteer coordinator for the annual live nativity.

"I'm supposed to be preaching that night," Devon said.

"I'll do it," I said.

"Awesome, I'll put you down. Maybe I can make you, Mom, and Lisa the three wise men." She laughed as she walked away with my bouquet.

"You ready?" Devon asked.

"Ready as I'll ever be," I said as cheerfully as I could muster.

I barely heard a word he said on our ride over to the apartment. The only thing I could think about was breaching the subject of divorce.

"You okay?" he asked when I hadn't acknowledged

what he said. "We don't have to go to our—my—house if you don't want to."

"No, it's okay. I was just—" I scrambled to think of an excuse "—admiring how much the landscape has changed."

He looked around at the splattering of homes built over the past ten years.

"Do we live in one of those homes?" I asked.

He frowned. "We live in an apartment. A pastor's salary isn't much."

As much as I wanted to be angry that we lived in such a teeny apartment, this was the first time he sounded embarrassed about how much he made. When *Love in Reality* had wrapped, he had gotten offer after offer for television hosting jobs, modeling jobs, even a newscaster position, but he had turned them all down. His focus was God, not fame and fortune.

"I'm sure it's a wonderful apartment," I said.

"If it is, it's only because of you. I'm no good at making a house a home."

He turned the car into the parking lot of our building.

"Here we are." He hurried around to my side of the car to open the door for me.

"Thank you." I took his hand to keep from slipping on the ice.

The minute we walked through the door to our apartment, my body froze. The smell of home made my eyes tear up. As tiny as it was, I missed it.

He turned to look at me. "It's overwhelming, I'm sure."

I nodded, not trusting my voice. How was I going to

ask for a divorce when every part of me was opposed to it?

God, give me the strength to do this. Devon deserves a wife who can be his perfect helper. The church deserves a woman who thrives on serving. And I deserve to be happy too.

"I'm not much of a cook, but I made spaghetti." He led me to the small dining room table. "It used to be your favorite."

"Mmm," I said. "It smells delicious."

I did my best to walk around as if I didn't know every creak in the floor. As if I wasn't surprised at how clean everything was.

"God, I thank you for Clara," Devon began before we ate. "Thank you for her smile. The way she loves You. And for giving us a second chance when You could have called her home that night. In Your precious name I pray, amen."

"Amen," I repeated. He could have prayed for me to regain my memories. He could have prayed that I'd fall back in love with him. But instead, he thanked God for my life. For a second chance.

"How is it living with Mrs. Wilton?" Devon asked as we slurped noodles into our mouths with sounds of delight.

"It's not bad. She's wonderful, you know?" I said. "Of course, you do. You've known her these past few years, right?"

"She's practically a grandmother to me," he said.

"She seems to have that effect on people. Every day with her is a true blessing."

"And was your first day of work a good one?"

"It was," I said. "I never knew how much fun it could be to work in a bookstore. I thought I'd be a librarian or something, but the bookstore is so much better. I get to talk to customers, recommend books, and I don't have to do a bunch of re-shelving. After decorating, though, I am a bit sore."

"I bet you are," he said. "But it sounds great. Very low key."

"I'm not sure what being a pastor's wife was like, but I'm loving this job."

"Being a pastor's wife is one of the hardest jobs in the world, I think. Possibly even harder than being a pastor."

"How so?" I asked.

"The pastor's wife has to deal with all the little things. All the socialization, the random meetings, the parishioners. You didn't get much time for yourself, and it definitely wasn't low key."

"It sounds like something Lisa would be good at."

"Lisa probably would be," he said. "But God didn't call her to the role like he called you."

I nearly spit out my water. "You think God called me to be a pastor's wife?"

"Yes," he said. "I'm certain he wouldn't have called me to be a pastor if you weren't meant to be a pastor's wife."

I'd never considered that.

"But pastor's wives have different functions in all the churches, right?" I asked.

"Sure," he said.

"How did I get the duties I had?"

"I think most of them were out of necessity. And you're so good at anything you put your mind to. It's like the door-to-door ministry. You hated the thought of it until you started talking to people. Listening to them.

Most of our parishioners are in the pews every Sunday because of how welcoming you are."

Why did he have to say such nice things now?

"And the Bible study?" I asked.

"That was a suggestion from the board," he said.

From Judy to be more accurate.

"Why would the board suggest I lead a Bible study?"

"They recognized the need in our church. Women aren't connecting. And they thought you'd be the perfect person to bring them all together."

Me? I had so many questions, but I couldn't ask them. If I did, he'd know I was faking.

"For what it's worth, I'm sorry you have to go through this," I said, looking past him at the photo we had taken in the Bahamas. We seemed so happy. Tan. Glowing.

He followed my gaze. "That was a fun trip," he said. "It's too bad you don't remember it." He took the last bite of his food and wiped his mouth.

"Can you tell me about it?"

"We hadn't ever taken an actual vacation. Not together anyway." He pulled the picture off the wall and looked at it lovingly. "You found a great deal and practically had to beg me to go. I can be stubborn about how we spend our money. But if I'd have known this would happen, I would have taken you on a million trips."

I stood and picked up our empty plates. He had always been able to read my emotions.

"The Bahamas were beautiful. The water was as blue as I've ever seen. And there was food—so much food—day and night. We could swim up to a pizza shack right in the middle of the pool. And we were so happy."

"It sounds wonderful." I rinsed the dishes and loaded them into the dishwasher.

"You don't have to clean." He replaced the photo on the wall. "I can get it later."

"No, it's okay," I said. "I don't mind." It felt good to be back in my own kitchen.

"One night in the Bahamas, we were down on the beach laying in hammocks."

I remembered that night vividly.

"The breeze was just enough to wash away any stagnant fishy smells. We held hands rocking back and forth, talking about our deepest fears and biggest dreams."

"What were mine?" I asked.

He gulped. "You said your fear was being taken advantage of by your friends, by your family, by me."

I could add the church to that list.

"And my dream?"

He shifted in his seat. "To have lots and lots of babies."

I replaced the hand towel on the bar of the oven door. "And what were yours?"

"My biggest fear was failing as a pastor. We were just starting the church at that point, and I had terrible imposter syndrome."

"But you don't now?" I asked.

He stood, and we walked into the living room, taking our usual seats.

"Not so much anymore," he said. "It's getting easier. Though not having you as a sounding board has been hard this week. You usually listen to me practice my sermons."

"I do?" I asked.

"I find the more I practice, the fewer mistakes I make."

"Do you think maybe practicing is relying too much on your own skill and not relying enough on the Holy Spirit?"

He looked as taken aback as I felt.

Where had those words come from?

"I've never thought of it like that," he said. "I've always been a performer, I guess. And I think part of the reason they gave me the job in the first place was because I was a faux-lebrity."

"A faux-lebrity?" I laughed. "What's that?"

"Like a fake celebrity. I don't really have any celebrity power, but people know my face as that guy they saw somewhere."

And he was incredibly handsome. Women probably dragged themselves out of bed every Sunday morning just to get an eyeful.

He'd have no problem finding a new wife. A lump rested in my throat at the thought.

"Devon, there's something I need to talk to you about."

I had to do it. My heart was softening. If I didn't do it now, I would lose my nerve.

"I'm all ears," he said, his smile faltering a bit.

"You seem wonderful. And it sounds like we were really happy," I said. "But—"

At that moment, my phone rang from inside my jacket pocket hanging by the front door.

"That's Lisa's ring," he said.

"It's pretty late for her to be calling." I ran to grab my phone. "Hello?"

"Clara?" Lisa's voice was strained.

"Is it time?" I asked.

"It's time. And I want you here with me."

Excitement rose in my chest. "We'll be right there."

"We?" Lisa said before letting out a hissing exhale.

"Devon and me. We were having dinner," I said.

"See you soon," she said before disconnecting the line.

"Lisa's having her baby," I said. "Can you take me to the hospital?"

He already had his shoes on.

Our talk would have to wait.

Three sets of tiny arms circled my waist when we walked into the hospital.

"Auntie Clara!"

Their sweet voices made me smile.

Dan pulled their twins—Autumn and Haley—back and Blake pulled Jacob—Lisa's little boy—back.

"Auntie Clara is having a hard time remembering," Blake said with a smile. "Let's not overwhelm her."

I crouched down to look at them. "I may not remember, but I am positive I loved you," I said, holding my arms out for another round of hugs.

"How's Lisa?" Devon asked.

"Don't know," Dan said. "She started having contractions about an hour ago, and they rushed here. We haven't heard anything since they took her back."

"Should we go sit down?" I asked the kids.

They nodded and pulled me over to where they had

already created a little nest of their jackets and hats and gloves. Blake, Dan, and Devon followed.

"Can we pray for Aunt Lisa, Mommy?" I asked, and all the kids nodded and clasped hands.

Usually, I would have let Devon pray—he was the pastor after all—but I took the opportunity to pray myself.

"Jesus, we thank You so much for the gift of life. Your sweet love gave us these beautiful children. You knit them together in their mothers' wombs, and I can't wait to meet the newest addition to this beautiful little tribe. Please bless me with children of my own someday, but for now, thank You for the gift of these little faces. Be with Lisa and Nathan and this new baby. Give the doctors and nurses wisdom. And be with us as we wait. Thank You, Jesus. Amen."

Little amens sounded around me along with those mumbled from the adults. Devon turned away from me to look out the window at the dark landscape. I could have sworn there was a glint of tears in his eyes, but I may have imagined it.

Minutes passed, then hours, and by the time we heard anything, I had three little children sleeping on me. Jacob was curled up in my lap like a cat, and Blake's twins sat on either side of me, their heads resting on my sides.

"Hey, guys," Lisa's calm voice whispered as she walked into the waiting room.

Devon and Dan stood up.

"What happened?" Blake asked, her voice hushed, so she didn't wake up the kids.

"False alarm." Lisa blushed. "This baby still needs to cook a little longer."

CHAPTER 10

*D*evon and I didn't speak as he drove me back to Mrs. Wilton's building. After the excitement of the night, we were both tired.

"Thanks for everything," I said when he pulled up to the building.

He put the car in park and turned to face me. "Do you want me to walk you up?"

"Nah, I'll be okay," I said with a smile.

"I know right now might not be the time to bring this up, but I'm here to chat whenever you want to revisit the subject we were about to broach when you got Lisa's call."

My heart constricted. "Maybe when I'm not so tired."

He nodded. I could see fear in his eyes, but he was never one to push me into discussing hard topics.

"I should probably get upstairs. I have to work early tomorrow."

"Before you go," he said as I reached for the door handle. "Do you think you and I could get together again tomorrow? Not so much as a date, but I'd really like to run my sermon by you."

"Sure, I'll listen, but only once. Then I think you should put it away and let the Holy Spirit guide you on Sunday."

"But—"

"No but," I said with a smile. "If you want my help, you'll agree to my terms."

He sat gaping at me for a beat before he nodded once. "Agreed."

"Then I'll see you tomorrow." I was almost excited to hear one of his sermons.

The light of day peeked through my curtains much too early. The smell of coffee in the kitchen was the only thing enticing me to get out of bed. Well, and the fact that I had to work. At least as a stay-at-home pastor's wife, I got to sleep in occasionally.

Mrs. Wilton sat at the kitchen table next to a small red-headed girl, and a woman with the longest legs I'd ever seen stood at the stove making eggs.

"Good morning," Mrs. Wilton said. "Gracie, this is Clara."

The little girl held out her hand, and I shook it. "It's a pleasure to meet you, Gracie."

"Yes," she said, then went back to the coloring book in front of her.

"And this is my daughter, Nelly," Mrs. Wilton said.

Nelly smiled and shook my hand. "I've heard a lot about you," she said, her voice clipped.

Mrs. Wilton frowned a bit when she said that. What exactly had she told her?

"It's been wonderful of your mom to take me under her wing as I recover from the accident."

"Amnesia must suck," she said, sliding a plate of eggs in front of Mrs. Wilton.

"It's not great," I said. "I thought you weren't going to be in town for another week."

"We had a change of plans. A job I'd booked fell through."

I took a moment to look at her more closely. Everything about her screamed high-fashion. Her cheekbones were pointy, her clothes were designer, and her blonde hair was as silky as the people in the shampoo commercials. But wrinkles peeked out from the corners of her eyes.

"So, you're a pastor's wife?"

"I was when I remembered." I glanced at Mrs. Wilton. Apparently, she hadn't let Nelly in on my secret. "Right now, I work in the children's section of the local bookstore."

"Sounds boring," she said.

"Many people might think so," I said, trying to laugh my way past her thinly veiled insult. "But I love this little town. In high school, I was never the girl who yearned to leave. I always knew I'd end up here."

"You never wanted to travel?" Nelly asked.

"I've done my fair share of traveling as a missionary. I don't remember it, though."

She wrinkled her nose but said nothing more.

"You look great this morning," I said to Mrs. Wilton.

"When Nelly and Gracie showed up, it was like the sun came out." She squeezed the little girl who giggled. They'd become close so quickly.

"How was your date with Devon?" she asked.

"It was okay."

"Did you let him down easy?"

"I didn't have time to bring it up," I said. "Lisa had a false alarm at the hospital, and it pushed everything else to the back burner."

"Mom says you're going to divorce your husband." Nelly sat down next to her daughter, not bothering to ask if I wanted coffee or eggs. Not that it was her job to wait on me. I stood and got my own coffee.

"I'm not sure who he is," I said. "I have no memory of him."

"But still, he's your husband."

I wanted to ask where Gracie's father was—Nelly wasn't wearing a ring—but thought better of it.

Judge not.

Though I was already being judged.

"Don't you want children?" Nelly asked.

"I do," I said. "I've decided to adopt once the divorce is final, and I've settled into life."

"Being a single mother is nothing to take lightly." Nelly ran a hand over Gracie's hair.

"It's better than not having kids at all." I shrugged and took a sip of my coffee. "I never thought I'd be in my thirties without kids."

Nelly shrugged but said nothing else.

"I should probably head out so I'm not late for work," I said, standing. "It was wonderful meeting you both."

"Maybe tonight you and Gracie could work together to decorate the apartment for Christmas," Mrs. Wilton said.

"I'm helping Devon with something right after work, but when I get home, I'd love to help decorate."

Gracie bounced in her chair with a big smile.

Yes, being a single mother would be far better than never having a child at all.

Work passed in the blink of an eye. It was amazing how much fun it could be to earn a paycheck doing something you loved. Even if it was boring by New York City standards.

I drove straight from work to the church where Devon said he wanted to go over the sermon.

Butterflies fluttered in my stomach when I thought about seeing him. I tensed my stomach muscles, trying—unsuccessfully—to crush them.

Darn butterflies.

A smile breached my lips. How long had it been since I'd felt butterflies for Devon? Maybe I'd just tell Devon the truth, beg him for children.

I shook my head. That was a bit drastic. He might not even take me back knowing I'd lied to him.

He wasn't in his office when I walked in. Maybe he was going to meet me in the sanctuary.

Sure enough, he was standing at the podium.

"You're not practicing, are you?" I asked, my voice teasing.

He looked up from his notes. "Nope. I made a promise," he said. "But I was starting to think you might not come."

"I don't know who I am in the present day," I said. "But I don't like to break promises."

"You're just as honorable as you were back then," he said. "Before I begin, I'd like to know if you're okay with me talking about you during my sermon? Your accident and everything?"

I hesitated. I didn't much like people knowing about my weaknesses.

"If you don't want me to, I won't. I can leave those parts out."

I sat in the very first row of chairs, front and center. "Why don't you include them in your practice run, and if I don't like them, I'll give you another practice run without them?"

"Deal."

"Then proceed," I said. Habit made me reach for my phone, but I stopped myself. I was here to listen, not pretend.

Devon began with a prayer and scripture and then launched into the story. "As many of you already know, my wife was in a car accident this past week. Though she's still with us, praise God, she has completely forgotten the past ten years. She has completely forgotten me."

He paused to regain his composure.

"And as hard as that's been, it's also opened my eyes.

It's given me the opportunity to win my wife's heart for a second time. But what if she doesn't want it?" He glanced down at his notes. "I'm tempted to push, to force my love on her, to do all sorts of things to prove I'm the guy for her. But as I was about to call her the other day, I heard God say, 'Do not force your love,' and it made me think about how God doesn't force His love on us. He gives us the ability to choose to love Him. And with that ability comes a relationship far deeper than it would be if he forced it on us."

My heart was beating so loudly I could hear it in my chest.

"Could I point to our marriage certificate and demand that she move back in with me? She's a God-fearing woman and would likely do just that."

I probably wouldn't, but I wasn't going to interrupt him.

"But if I did, I'd never know if she was there because she loved me or because I'd forced her. God will not force you to love Him. To listen to Him. He's a gentleman. He'll knock on the door to your heart, but He won't bust it down. You have to open it."

He paused for effect.

"Don't get me wrong. I'm not comparing myself to God. I'm simply considering how there have been times I've forced my way with things when I should have stood back and let God do his thing."

He smiled at me.

"If you turn in your Bible to . . ."

The rest of the sermon was perfect. Completely on

point. When he finished with the final prayer, I stood up and clapped.

He laughed. "That's the first time anyone's ever clapped for one of my sermons."

"You were great." I walked up on stage and stood next to him. "Now," I took the notes off the podium, folded them, and slipped them inside his jacket pocket. "Don't take these out again until Sunday."

He looked uneasy but nodded.

"I'm starving. We should get a bite to eat," he said. "How's the weather?"

"It's not too cold," I said.

"Warm enough to walk?"

"How far are we walking?"

"There's this little place on the corner you've loved since it opened. It's called the Cantina. It has the best green chili in the state."

My mouth instantly watered, we hadn't been to the Cantina in forever. "It sounds wonderful."

We put on our coats and hats and scarves, locked the church, and walked side by side down the sidewalk.

White twinkle lights formed big spirals down the lampposts lining the street. Shops had Christmas trees in their windows. Big snowflakes fell lazily from the sky, landing on the tip of my nose before melting.

"It's a beautiful night," I said.

"Yeah, it is," Devon said, but he wasn't looking at anything but me.

I could feel the blush rise in my cheeks.

We rounded a corner, and my gaze rested on the place

that held my heart—my parents' old house. "I can't believe they sold the house."

"It looks like whoever bought it sold it again." Devon pointed to the for sale sign with a sold sticker on top in the yard.

My stomach dropped. If only I had known.

Then what? There's no way I would have been able to afford it. My job at the bookstore only paid minimum wage.

I stood frozen on the spot staring at the place where I'd had some of the happiest times in my life. Not that I hadn't been happy with Devon, but my childhood was practically a dream. My childhood home was my dream home. "I want to go inside," I whispered.

Devon interlaced his fingers through mine. "Then let's go," he said. "What's the worst they can say? No?"

I hesitated. He'd never been so spontaneous. "You're right. If they say no, it's not the end of the world."

He led me up the newly refinished and shoveled wood steps that opened up to the wrap-around porch and a turquoise front door. It had been brown when I was a kid, but the turquoise was nice too.

The bell I'd heard hundreds of times chimed when Devon pushed the button. I remembered Blake and Lisa ringing the bell to pick me up for school or shopping. My first boyfriend ringing it and my father insisting he answer it instead of me. I rang the same bell the night Devon had proposed. My parents had known the moment they opened the door.

"Can I help you?" A woman in her early to mid-sixties opened the door.

"My wife used to live here as a child, and we'd like to know if we could come in for just a few minutes?"

The woman's face cracked into a smile. "Of course, my dear," she said. "It's sold, but the new owners won't take possession for another couple of weeks."

She opened the door and led us inside. The paint was different, hardwood floors had replaced the shag carpet, but the staircase still gently slid from the second floor into the foyer. Pillows and a soft blanket filled the bay window where I'd read hundreds of books growing up.

"You say you lived here as a child?" she asked.

I nodded. "I think you bought the house from my parents a few years ago?"

Devon spoke up. "Clara was in a car accident and has amnesia."

"Oh yes, I heard about you. Judy was talking about it at tea the other morning."

Leave it to Judy to make me the talk of the town.

"I do hope you get better soon," she said, looking at Devon. "Can I show you around the house?"

The doorframe where my father had measured each of my siblings and me on the first day of school still had our markings. I ran my hand over them.

Tears welled in my eyes.

My breaths were short and labored.

If only I'd known it was for sale. I would have bought it. Somehow. I would have made it work. Now some other family would raise their kids in my house.

"Are you okay?" Devon asked.

"Thank you for inviting us in," I said as evenly as I could. "But I think I should go."

I turned and left before the sweet woman could stop me. Cold air felt like daggers in my lungs.

"I'm sorry," Devon said to the woman.

"It perfectly okay," the woman said.

Devon came to stand by my side as I struggled to take deep breaths. He rubbed circles on my back.

"Are you okay?" he asked.

I turned and buried my face into his chest. For a second, he didn't move, but then he wrapped his arms around me. "It'll be okay."

"I can't believe I didn't even try to buy this house," I said into his chest. "Did I know it was for sale?"

"I don't think so," Devon answered.

We stood there long enough for me to have a good cry. I finally pulled away and wiped the tears from my face. "Let's get some food."

He smiled. "Yes, let's."

The Cantina smelled heavenly when we walked in. I was hungrier than I thought. The short walk from my childhood home to the Cantina allowed me to regain my thoughts and wrangle my tears.

"Thanks again for helping me with my sermon."

"It was my pleasure," I said. "I'm only sad I won't be there to hear it."

"You're not coming to church on Sunday?"

I shook my head. "I'm going to the pre-Christmas retreat at the Big Mountain Lodge and Resort."

"Good," he said. "I didn't know if you'd still want to go with everything that happened."

"I didn't want to waste the money you—we—spent on it. Plus, it sounds like it'll be fun."

"I think you'll have a great time."

I smiled and savored a bite of chips and salsa. "What was your favorite part of being a missionary?"

"That's tough." He thought for a moment. "Seeing people saved and the miracles of healing were wonderful, but honestly, when I look back on those days, all I remember is being with you." His grin was sheepish. "Cheesy, I know. But it's true. I can remember the way you smiled when you saw a giraffe in the wild for the first time. Or when you laid hands on a little girl and prayed so fervently for her that God restored her hearing."

I could picture that moment. It had been wonderful. "Do you ever want to go back to being a missionary?"

"Tough questions tonight," he said with a smile. "I don't think so. Not like we were, anyway. I'm glad we're settling into our lives here with the church and all."

The waitress delivered two big bowls of green chili and a plate of warm tortillas.

"Oh my goodness, this looks amazing," I said. "Thank you."

She nodded and took our drinks to refill.

I eagerly took a bite and burned my tongue. "Ooh ouch."

"What? What's wrong?" Devon almost stood.

"Nothing." I laughed. "It's just hot."

He laughed too.

"Hot but delicious," I said. "I've missed this."

His eyebrows furrowed together in the middle of his forehead.

"I mean green chili. It's not quite as good as—"

"Your mother's." His face returned to normal. "You say that every time we're here."

"But it's pretty close."

We ate in silence until we had practically licked our bowls clean.

"Thank you for bringing me here," I said. "I think I needed some food. I was getting overly emotional."

"About the house?" he asked.

I nodded. "I shouldn't have gotten so worked up."

"You don't need to apologize. I completely understand. When you found out your parents were selling it originally, you cried for days."

I remembered.

"I'd say you're taking it rather well this time," he said. "Shall we?"

I stood and put on my heavy winter attire again. "Thank you again. This was really nice."

"It was my pleasure. I can't remember the last time we did something like this," he said. "I just keep kicking myself for all the things I didn't do when you had your memory."

We'd fallen into the married couple rut. Working every waking hour for the church didn't leave much time for us.

"Can I tell you a secret?" he asked.

"Sure."

"The night I found out you were okay after the accident, but you had lost your memory, I was almost relieved."

"Relieved? Why?" Did he want a divorce too? Maybe this was an answer to both of our prayers. My chest tightened, but I pushed the feeling down. It was for the best.

"Because I wanted a chance to start fresh," he said.

I didn't know what to say. I couldn't believe he was doing this now. After the night we'd had. I mean, I was going to say it too, but I was the one who'd lost my memory, not him. And how would he explain it to the church? He'd definitely lose his job.

We walked in silence for a couple of blocks.

"Did I say something wrong?" he finally asked.

"No." I took a deep breath. "I think it's good that we're both on the same page. I'll talk to an attorney and have them write up the divorce agreement."

"Divorce agreement?" Devon stopped walking. "What do you mean divorce agreement?"

"You said you wanted to start fresh," I said. "And since I don't remember you . . ."

"I meant start fresh with *you*," he said. "I don't want to start fresh with anyone else."

Oh.

"You must have been so confused when I said that," he said.

"I wouldn't blame you if that's what you wanted."

"That's the furthest thing from what I want." He grabbed both of my hands in his and looked down into my eyes. "I wasn't a great husband. Far from it. When you got in your accident, I was relieved it took away your memories of how awful I was. I was hopeful for a second chance with you."

Why did he have to say such melty words when I needed to tell him we had to get a divorce?

His eyes sparkled in the Christmas lights. I wanted so badly to kiss him. To fall into his arms and start fresh.

But I couldn't.

I dropped his hands. "I should get back. Thank you again for dinner."

I could feel him watching me as I walked away.

racie sat in the middle of the living room floor, surrounded by boxes and boxes of Christmas decorations when I walked in the door.

"Yay! You're here!" Gracie jumped to her feet and pulled me to where she'd been sitting.

I slapped a smile on my face and pushed away the mixed-up feelings in my head.

"How was your time with Devon?" Mrs. Wilton asked from the dining room table where she and Nelly huddled over a stack of paperwork.

"It was okay," I said, not wanting to get into the details. "Shall we decorate?" I usually loved decorating, but I just wanted to get this going so we could get it over with, and I could go to bed.

"Let's do the tree," Gracie said.

While I'd been gone, they'd set up a small fake tree in the corner but had left it bare. Growing up, we always had real trees. Sure they made a mess, but the smell was something a candle couldn't recreate.

Gracie examined each ornament I handed her before finding the perfect spot for it on the tree. It took longer, but her slow, repetitive motions calmed me.

Mrs. Wilton and Nelly were off in their own world, talking in whispers I knew had nothing to do with me. Even if I tried, I wouldn't have been able to make out what they were saying.

"Will you lift me up to put the angel on top of the tree?" Gracie asked.

The angel she held in her hands was gorgeous. With a white silk dress, wings, a halo, and a small candle held between her hands. She looked exactly the way most people pictured angels.

I grabbed Gracie by the waist and lifted her as high as I could.

"Have you seen the tree in the town square?" I asked.

She shook her head, no.

"You should definitely see it before you leave. It's beautiful."

Gracie's eyes twinkled. "I love Christmas."

"What's your favorite part?" I asked.

"The lights. Or maybe the cookies." She thought for a moment. "No, definitely the lights."

"I like the lights too."

We finished with a few other touches—a Santa here, a nutcracker there—before we stood back to examine our handiwork.

"I'd say we did a pretty good job." I high-fived Gracie.

"Pretty good?" Mrs. Wilton said from behind us. "This place looks magical."

Gracie bounded over and jumped up on her lap, giving her grandmother a huge hug.

Nelly shuffled the papers together and deposited them into a large purse next to her.

"I should probably go to bed," I said. "Thank you so much for your help tonight, Gracie. I couldn't have done it without you."

"You're welcome," Gracie said in her sweet little voice.

The next morning, I got up early, packed a small bag, and took a taxi to the Big Mountain Lodge and Resort. The retreat didn't officially begin until ten, but they served some of the best cappuccinos in the world.

I settled into an oversized chair in front of a grand stone fireplace decorated with fresh pine sprigs and warm white lights. A Christmas tree that reached two stories to the peaked ceiling was decorated in blue and silver with a sparkly star on top. Gracie would have loved it. I sipped my drink and imagined what Christmas would be like this year.

My parents would still be on their cruise, meaning I'd be decorating the cabin alone. Usually Devon helped me, but I couldn't rely on his help anymore. I had to do things myself.

"Clara?" Blake's voice came from the other side of the room.

"Hey," I said.

"You're here early," she looked at her watch. "The retreat doesn't begin for another couple of hours."

"I know," I said. "I couldn't sleep, and I needed some coffee." I held up my cup.

"I see you found our world-famous cappuccino," she said. "Best kept secret this side of the Mississippi."

"It's delicious," I agreed. "How are the preparations going?"

She wore a headset you almost couldn't see through her thick curls.

"Everything's in order. The staff does all the work. It's more of a formality for me to have a headset."

And a sign of the perfectionist inside her.

"It's so cool you own this place," I said. "And you have Dan and kids. You're doing so well as an adult."

"I have my days," she said. "How are you and Devon? It was kind of nice seeing the two of you together at the hospital the other night."

"We're—I don't know—it's complic—"

"Yeah?" Blake said, staring above my head while she pressed a button on the side of her headset. "I'll be right there." She returned her attention to me. "Sorry, there's a minor emergency. We can talk later, okay?"

I nodded and tried to smile as she walked away, her heels clicking on the floor.

As the sun rose, more and more women meandered into the lodge den to get their coffee. I recognized nearly all of them from church, but they steered clear of me. I guess since they thought I didn't remember, they figured they didn't need to bring me into the loop.

About fifteen minutes before the retreat was supposed to begin, Lisa waddled in and sat next to me.

"How are you?" I asked.

"I'm huge," Lisa said without so much as a smile. "This baby needs to make her exit. Pronto."

I'd never been pregnant, but I'd always heard the last month was the longest. "Can I get you something to drink?"

"Water only." She held up a huge water bottle. "How are you and Devon?"

"We're okay," I said. "We hung out last night."

"Two nights in a row, huh?" she smiled. "Have you gotten any of your memories back?"

"Not yet."

"That's too bad."

"Hey guys." Blake plopped down in one of the open seats near us. She wasn't wearing a headset anymore. "Are you ready to get this party started?"

Lisa and I nodded, though my nod was notably more excited than Lisa's.

A young woman made her way to the front of the crowd, and when she spoke, her voice reverberated through the room. "Hello everyone."

Blake watched her employee like a hawk. She was one of the best event planners in the country and was training her staff to be just as meticulous as she had been when she was at the helm.

"This will be a great weekend."

Claps and small cheers sounded around me.

"With just over a week left until Christmas, I'm sure

we could all use a little rest and relaxation . . . and shopping, of course."

The women giggled excitedly. I couldn't help but smile.

"But on top of all that, we will have some amazing sessions specifically geared to encourage and uplift you no matter what season of life you're in."

My gaze was pulled to the doorway where Judy and Sydney had snuck in. My spirits sank. I hadn't considered they'd be here. But of course, they would. The church sponsored a large portion of this retreat.

"The registration tables will open the moment I'm finished speaking so you can get your room assignments and schedules. Feel free to go to whatever sessions you want. There are no rules this weekend. We just want you to go into this holiday season with as much joy as you can."

It sounded lovely. I'd just have to avoid Sydney and Judy at all costs.

CHAPTER 12

"*N*ame?" the woman at one of the registration tables asked when it was my turn.

"Clara Langly," I said.

The woman getting registered next to me raised an eyebrow. "Don't you have amnesia?"

She had only been to our church once or twice. "I do. Why?"

"Your name rolled off your tongue pretty easily," she accused.

"I've been—uh—practicing saying it. Since the accident. Trying to get a feel for it, you know?" I smiled, trying not to give away my secret. "Sometimes, I watch myself in the mirror and recite it over and over again."

Lies, lies, and more lies.

"Mrs. Langly," the registration lady interrupted. "Here is your room key and your gift pack. Feel free to take everything to your room. We will have lunch at eleven-thirty, and the retreat will begin shortly after."

The gift bag was a small duffle bag that probably weighed twenty pounds.

"Thank you," I said, hurrying away before I was questioned further.

My room was on the tenth floor, west side. I'd have a great view of the sunset.

Lisa, Blake, and I agreed to meet back in the lobby around eleven-fifteen so we could sit together for lunch. I steered clear of Sydney and Judy as I made my way to the tenth floor.

When I opened the door to my room, I nearly dropped my bags. This couldn't be right.

I glanced down at the room number to confirm I was in the right place. The numbers matched.

Pink rose petals covered the floor and the enormous king-sized bed. A huge bouquet of pink roses sat on the desk near the window that showcased the Rocky Mountains in all their glory. An envelope with my name on it leaned against the lamp on the nightstand.

Clara,

I hope you have fun this weekend.
Here is some cash for you to spend.
I love you.

Yours,
Devon

Several hundred-dollar bills fell from inside the envelope. Since when did Devon dole out cash like he was some sort of ATM? And the flowers must have cost a fortune. I couldn't accept all this, not when I was prepared to leave him. But I knew he'd be disappointed if I didn't spend at least a little bit of the money. I shoved it into the pocket of my jeans.

The small duffle bag was next on my list. What could weigh so much inside?

When I opened the zipper, items practically spilled out.

Bath bombs, lotions, soaps, candles, a bracelet from the local jewelry store, hair accessories, a sleep mask, and a silky robe with my initials monogrammed on the chest. Where had they gotten all this? Surely the church hadn't paid for it, and I know the cost of attending the retreat wouldn't cover it.

I opened the envelope enclosed.

Thank you for attending the first annual Ladies' Christmas Retreat. Our local community partners have been incredibly generous, donating so many amazing items to the gift bags to help make you feel extra special. Each of these partners will have pop-up shops set up in the main ballroom where you can do some last-minute Christmas shopping.

Also, please enjoy these complimentary vouchers for a massage, manicure, and pedicure. The spa is open twenty-four hours a day, seven days a week. You can also visit the pool, fitness center, steam room, and Jacuzzi tubs at your convenience.

We hope you have a very blessed Christmas and enjoy your stay at the Big Mountain Lodge and Resort.

I'd never seen so many amazing things in my life. Giddiness crept up my chest. I slipped the bracelet on my wrist and checked my phone for the time. I'd have to hurry back downstairs to meet Lisa and Blake for lunch, but so much of me wanted to relax in this magnificent room and enjoy all the sweet gifts.

"I'll be back soon," I said to no one as I closed the door on the scent of roses.

"Who are you talking to?" Judy's voice came from behind me.

I nearly jumped out of my skin. Thankfully, I didn't scream. "You scared the living daylights out of me."

"You didn't answer my question." Judy stood with her hands on her hips, eyebrows raised. "I know you weren't talking to Devon. He and Vern are in a meeting as we speak."

"Oh," I said. "I wasn't talking to anyone. It's stupid—I was talking to my room."

Judy just stared at me.

"I'm telling the truth," I said.

She still said nothing.

Part of me wanted to open the door and let her inside to see for herself, but I didn't need to explain myself to Judy. Not anymore.

"Believe me or don't," I said. "I have to get down to lunch. My friends are waiting for me." I walked away, leaving Judy probably still standing there staring at me like a wicked statue.

"Finally," Lisa said when I got to them in the lobby. "I'm starving."

"Sorry, I had a little run-in with Judy," I said just as Judy stormed past me, mumbling under her breath.

"What did you do this time?" Blake asked with a laugh.

"I said goodbye to my room—which is gorgeous, by the way—and she thought someone was inside," I said.

"Did you show her there wasn't?" Blake asked as we followed Lisa to the buffet line.

"No. I don't have to prove anything to Judy. She's not the boss of me." I sounded like a child, but I was in the right here, not her.

Blake lifted her hands in surrender. "I agree. You owe her nothing."

"Oh my goodness, these tiny sausages are amazing," Lisa said, devouring the food as fast as she put it on her plate.

Once everyone finished their meals, the same woman from this morning stood up on a platform and spoke into a mic. "I hope your lunch was as delicious as mine. Can we give the kitchen staff a round of applause, please?"

Applause erupted from what I estimated to be one to two hundred women.

"Now that we're all fed, we're going to start some breakout groups. If you look at your schedules, you'll find the list of the first set of groups."

We opened our folders and pulled out the schedule. The topics for the first breakout session were Parenting through the Holidays, Surviving Your In-Laws, What to do When You and Your Husband aren't Clicking, and How to have a Merry Christmas without Breaking the Bank.

"Which one are you going to?" Lisa asked me.

"I don't know," I said. "Maybe I'll just tag along to whichever one you're going to."

Lisa looked at Blake and then back at me. "We're going to the Parenting one." She paused. "You're free to come with us, but I think it might be kind of boring since you . . ."

"Don't have kids," I said, finishing the sentence she didn't want to.

"I'm sure it wouldn't be too bad," Blake said. "Maybe you could get tips for when you do have kids."

I cleared the lump in my throat. They were part of an exclusive group, and I wasn't. "That's okay." I smiled as convincingly as I could. "I'll go to one of the other ones. Maybe I should go to the husband one. Goodness knows we're not exactly clicking right now."

They both laughed nervously at my joke.

"Are you sure?" Blake asked.

"Absolutely." I waved a hand for them to go. "I'll see you afterward at the pop-up shops."

"Great," Lisa said. "Have fun."

And they walked away, leaving me feeling utterly lost.

The sessions had already begun by the time I'd gotten myself together and chosen one. I decided it probably wouldn't hurt to go to the husband one after all since it was the closest to the one I would need.

The room was dark as the speaker went over a slideshow presentation. It was probably best to stand in the back of the room so no one saw the local pastor's wife in the marriage class. Plus, then I could leave the moment they turned the lights back on.

The speaker talked about how hard the holidays could be on relationships and how easy it was to get out of sync with each other. Her suggestions to remedy the situation were to slow down and talk without any distractions, talk about the budget before it became an issue of contention, and give each other hugs every day.

At the last point, a woman huffed and walked out of the room. She, too, stood at the back, trying not to be noticed. It almost worked.

"Judy?" I asked when I was safely in the hallway.

Judy spun around and glared at me. "Are you following me? I went in there by accident. There is absolutely nothing wrong with my marriage."

It was my turn to be suspicious. "I'm not accusing you of anything," I said. "But even if you were having troubles, it would be okay. It's not like I will tell anyone."

"Oh yeah, right. You're just saying that so I won't tell Devon that you had another man in your room."

I tipped my head back and laughed. "Are you serious?" She didn't move. "Fine, come on."

I grabbed her hand and pulled her toward the elevator. She followed reluctantly.

"You don't have to drag me. I can walk perfectly fine on my own."

I let go of her and pushed the number ten.

"You know, this proves nothing," she said, her voice still filled with vile arrogance. "The man could have easily snuck out by now."

"I said goodbye to my room," I said as we stepped out of the elevator. "I'll show you why."

When I opened the door, the smell of roses hit me again. "See," I said. "Isn't it beautiful?"

Judy walked in careful not to step on any of the flower petals.

"My room didn't look like this," Judy said. "I didn't have roses."

"Devon did it for me," I said.

Judy sat on the end of the bed, looking defeated. "Vern would never do something like this for me."

Was she trying to get me to let my guard down? Was this a trap?

But when she looked up with tears in her eyes, my defenses melted. I sat down next to her. "Are you okay?"

"No," she said. "I'm not okay."

I didn't know what to do, so I patted her on the shoulder awkwardly.

"Vern doesn't love me anymore," she said. "He said he wants to leave me, but he can't because divorce is a sin."

"He told you he wants to leave you?" That was crazy. They'd been together for practically forever.

"We lead two separate lives. He avoids me at all costs."

"But at church, you seemed okay," I said, passing her a tissue.

"Even our best effort to act happy is only okay." She dabbed at her eyes. "Why am I telling you this?" She stood and smoothed her blouse down.

"It's okay," I said. "I won't say anything. Marriage is hard."

She glared back at me. "How would you know?"

CHAPTER 13

*L*isa and Blake chatted animatedly when I walked into the large conference hall filled with pop-up shops.

"How was your session?" Blake asked when she saw me approaching.

"It was okay," I said. "Kind of irrelevant since I don't remember being married. How was yours?"

"It was great," Lisa said. "It's stressful being a mom during the holidays. You want everything to be perfect for your sweet littles, but you—or more like I—have to remember that it's not about everything being perfect."

"Easier said than done," Blake patted Lisa gently on the back.

"Should we do some shopping?" I asked, glancing around at the Christmas-colored booths.

"Definitely," Lisa and Blake said at the same time, giggling afterward.

I did my best not to roll my eyes.

I followed behind them as they made their way from

stall to stall talking about how much their husbands or kids would like something. I wanted to get Devon something, but I had to act like I didn't know what to get him. I knew he would have loved one of the fancy silk ties or the old-fashioned shaving kit, but if I got one of those, my friends would know I was lying.

An hour and a half later, Lisa and Blake were completely loaded down with bags. I'd bought my parents a couple of things and Devon a tie that wouldn't quite match his style, but he'd appreciate it nonetheless.

"Maybe we should take our bags up to the rooms before the next session starts," Blake said.

Lisa froze.

"Do you need me to carry those for you?" I offered for the hundredth time.

Lisa didn't move.

"What's wrong?" I asked.

Blake's eyes widened. "I think her water just broke."

I looked down at the floor to find the blue carpet just a bit darker beneath Lisa's shoes.

I grabbed the bags out of her hands. "We need to get you to the hospital."

Lisa snapped out of it and started barking orders at everyone. "You—" she'd point to some random woman "—take our bags to the front desk and have them hold them for us."

The woman nodded and did exactly as she said.

"Blake, get your car and meet us up front."

Blake nodded and took off at a sprint.

"Clara, hold on to me, I think I feel a contraction coming ooohhhh—" she let out a scream that stopped most of the people still shopping in their tracks. Her nails dug into my arm, but I couldn't complain. By the look on her face, she was in far more pain than she could inflict on me.

Once the contraction was over, she said, "Get me to the car before I have another one. This baby is coming now."

As we were shuffling to the doors, I saw Judy eyeing me from a corner of the room. I didn't have time to think about her problems right now. I had to be there for my friend.

The moment we arrived, the nurses whisked Lisa away. I was just thankful she didn't have her baby in the car.

Blake and I sat in content silence until Nathan showed up. Blake gave him the run-down of what had happened, and he rushed back to the delivery room.

Almost an hour later, the nurse returned. "Lisa is ready for you."

"Already?" Blake asked.

"She's lucky her husband arrived in time," the nurse said. "The baby was already almost out."

We followed her back to the delivery room, where Lisa sat in bed, holding a tiny bundle in a fuzzy pink blanket.

"She came so fast," Blake said. "Are you doing okay?"

"It was the easiest birth I've had," Lisa said. "I didn't even have time to be in pain. She was ready to make her grand entrance."

"You look beautiful," I said. And she did. You wouldn't have guessed what she'd just been through.

"Do you want to hold her?" Lisa asked, handing me the most precious little girl in the world.

I cuddled her in my arms and smiled down at her tiny features.

"What's her name?" Blake asked, peeking over my shoulder.

"Isla." Lisa looked up at Nathan. He nodded, beaming at his wife.

"Hello Isla," I said, and she wrinkled her nose the tiniest bit. "She is the cutest baby I've ever seen."

I passed Isla to Blake, who held her as only a seasoned mommy could. And to think, just a few years ago, Blake hadn't even wanted children.

Lisa's husband kissed her on her head. "I'm going to get a soda," he said. "Give you time to chitchat."

"I'm sorry I ruined the rest of the retreat for you," Lisa said.

"You ruined nothing. We'll go back tonight and enjoy tomorrow," Blake said.

"I don't think I asked, but how are things going with Devon?" Lisa asked.

"They're going okay," I said. "We had dinner a few nights ago and then last night too. I was going to tell him we need to get a divorce, but I haven't gotten the nerve."

Lisa looked at Blake. "Sounds like a God thing."

Blake shrugged but smiled knowingly.

"He gave me permission to date Brian," I said.

"Who did?" Blake asked, keeping her voice low and sweet so as not to wake Isla. "Devon?"

I nodded.

"Is he nuts?" Blake looked like her face might explode. She placed Isla carefully back in Lisa's arms.

"I think he wants me to do what I need to do to get my memories back." I shifted my gaze from Blake to Lisa.

Lisa gave us a look of consternation. She was contemplating. When Blake realized Lisa wouldn't back her up, she continued. "Do you want me to help you remember?" Her voice was louder now that she wasn't holding the baby. "Brian left you. He told you you weren't enough. That you were holding him back."

"Was Brian in your hotel room?" Lisa asked as if the thought had just popped into her head.

"No," I said as quietly but as sternly as I could. "Of course not. I haven't seen Brian since he brought me lunch at work a few days ago."

"But you're planning on dating him?" Lisa asked.

I shrugged. "Maybe."

"I know you have amnesia, but you still have a brain," Blake blurted out. "You should use it."

I had never seen Blake so frustrated. She was usually the easy-going one.

"Help me out here," Blake said to Lisa.

"She's right," Lisa said to me in a tired but firm voice. "Brian doesn't deserve your time. And as a good Christian woman—which I know you are—you shouldn't consider dating anyone but your husband. You may not remember, but you married him. And what happens when you remember? You will feel terrible you dated someone else."

"Well, thanks for your opinions," I said, trying to keep the tears from my voice. My best friends were ganging up against me. They had no idea. "I think I'm going to head back to the resort." I turned toward the door. "Congratulations again. She's beautiful."

Neither of them stopped me.

I didn't see Blake the rest of my stay at her resort. This may or may not have been intentional.

Okay, it was intentional.

But it was also the room's fault.

It was so comforting, I didn't want to leave when Sunday afternoon rolled around.

I called a taxi from my room and left the room key on the dresser. I wasn't going to risk running into Blake checking out.

"Whoa, can I help you with some of that?" Judy asked as I emerged, juggling my bags and the flowers.

"Sure," I said. If I hadn't been so overloaded, I would have declined the offer.

"I'm sorry about yesterday," she said as we were getting into the elevator. "I should never have told you all that. It's not fair to put my burdens on you."

"I don't mind," I said.

"I appreciate that."

The cab was waiting when we walked out of the lobby.

"Thanks for your help," I said. "I'll see you around."

Judy nodded and handed me the vase of flowers.

I gave the taxi driver Mrs. Wilton's address, and he started down the long tree-lined driveway.

As the snowy scenery passed out the window, I decided to text Brian about going on that date.

He didn't return my text until well after ten o'clock that night. By that time, I'd climbed into my pajamas, said goodnight to Mrs. Wilton and Nelly, and was almost asleep.

But he said he wanted to pick me up in ten minutes.

Ten minutes? It was past ten.

He had probably been at the hospital all day.

I agreed.

CHAPTER 14

$\mathcal{M}$y mind was foggy with exhaustion when I climbed into Brian's red sports car.

"You look stunning," he said.

"Thanks," I said. I'd worn my cutest short skirt, black leggings, heels that made me at least three inches taller, and a blouse I could have never worn to church. It felt rebellious and exciting.

"How's your head?" he asked.

"I think it's almost healed. The stitches seem to be dissolving."

"And your memory?"

"If I had it, do you think I'd be hanging out with you tonight?"

"Point taken," he said with a laugh.

"We're going to my place, but not like you think," he said.

Brian was staying in one of the nicer condos in the town. Most of the tenants were millionaires but only visited on holidays and for ski breaks.

"We'll take the elevator," Brian said as he led me through the lobby. A massive double-sided fireplace sat in the middle of the room while families crowded around talking, playing games, and having a drink. "Christmas is a busy time for my building."

"I see." I did my best to smile. Why was everyone up so late? I was starting to feel my age.

The voices muffled into silence as the heavy elevator doors closed. He pushed the button for the top floor.

"You live on the roof?" I asked.

"I'm not taking you to my apartment. Too presumptuous. But the roof is the best place at this time of year."

I was seriously regretting my clothing choice. Even though it wasn't overly cold outside, a skirt would offer no protection.

"I have blankets," he said as if he'd read my mind.

The elevator doors opened to a simple landing and a stairwell. We walked up and out into the cold winter air.

White twinkle lights and cozy couches surrounded a sunken fire pit. The fire was warm. Brian wiped the snow from the cushions before turning them over so they'd be dry.

"Can I get you some hot cocoa?" he asked.

"Yes, thank you," I said.

He pulled out a thermos and two mugs.

"Why isn't anyone else up here?" I asked.

"I reserved it for the evening," he said.

His smile wasn't nervous or self-conscious. It was proud and almost boastful. He was the opposite of Devon in so many ways. The only thing they shared was their model-quality looks.

"So tell me more about these last few years," I said, hoping we could keep the conversation off me. "What have you been doing?"

He wrapped an arm around me. I leaned into his side as he started talking and didn't stop for what felt like forever. I didn't care much about where he'd been or what he was doing, but the warmth radiating from him and the hot cocoa soothed me. His voice was easy on the ears, even if I wasn't really listening.

"More hot cocoa?" he asked when he'd finished his story.

"I'm okay." I set my mug on the brick of the fire pit and standing up. He followed my lead to the edge of the roof. "Big Mountain is beautiful from up here."

He wrapped a blanket around my shoulders as he came to stand behind me. His arms crossed at my neck, and his chin rested on the top of my head. "It's even more beautiful with you."

"How long are you in town?" I asked.

"Until after Christmas," he said. "Mom and Dad would kill me if I left before Christmas. They'd love to see you, by the way."

His mom and dad had loved me until Brian and I had broken up. He told them I'd broken his heart, and that was why he moved to New York. "So, they've forgiven me?"

His biceps twitched. "You remember that?"

"I found out not too long after we broke up. Your mom called me."

"She didn't," he said, spinning me around to face him. "It was a stupid, cowardly move. I didn't want to be the bad guy. Dumping the perfect girl, leaving my family. It seemed so much easier to just—"

"Blame it on me," I finished.

He pulled me into a hug. "I'm sorry. I'll tell them the truth."

I pulled back. "You still haven't told them the truth? Was it a total lie when you said they'd love to see me?"

"I—no—well," he stuttered.

I gave him an intense stare before walking back to the fire pit. "I think I should go," I said, grabbing my purse.

"Please don't," he said. "I'm really sorry."

"Blake and Lisa told me not to see you. That you hadn't changed a bit. What else have you lied about?" I asked.

"You know I was engaged," he said, sitting down where we'd been before.

"Yes."

"She broke my heart. Into a million tiny pieces. It seemed like payback for what I did to you."

"Have you gotten over her?" I sat next to him.

"Yeah. I think so." He shrugged. "She's moved on. But I thought she was the one."

"I know the feeling," I mumbled.

"She reminded me so much of you, though."

"Didn't you say she was a model?"

"Yeah."

I looked at him, waiting for it to register that I was nowhere near model status. When he didn't say anything else, I said, "Have you dated much since?"

"Not really," he said. "Mostly just a few dates here and

there. I threw myself into work. Now I travel all over the United States consulting for hospitals."

"Like the one here in Big Mountain?"

"Yep. And it just so happened to be the exact time you ended up there. I'm usually all about coincidence, but that seemed planned somehow."

"You think God planned for us to meet?" I asked.

"God, the universe, whoever. But yeah," he said. "You lose your memory of your husband, and I happen to be the one standing next to your bed when you wake up?"

Technically, it had been a nurse there when I woke up but . . .

"Maybe this is our second chance." He cupped my face in his hands, bringing my gaze to his. "You're so beautiful. I've missed you so much."

He leaned in to kiss me.

Twenty-some-year-old Clara would have let him. She would have given in. She would have fallen right back into his arms.

But the closer he got, the more I felt like I was going to be sick.

I couldn't kiss him.

I put a hand to his chest. "I can't do this."

"What do you mean?" he asked. "Haven't you missed me? In your mind, it hasn't been that long since we broke up. You can't tell me you've gotten over me that quickly."

I shook my head. "Maybe I haven't, but I know I'm married. God knows I'm married. And until that's no longer the case, I need to stay true to myself." I stood up. "Thanks for the cocoa."

CHAPTER 15

The next day at work, Elaine had to run some errands leaving me in charge of the store for an hour or so.

The children's section was looking better by the day. I'd placed an order for some additional books to enhance the selection, and they were scheduled to arrive today.

When the bell on the door chimed, I thought it might be the mail delivery guy, but it wasn't. Judy stood at the front counter, tapping her fingernails on the polished wood.

"Hi, Judy. How are you?"

"I'm here to see Elaine." Any seedling of friendship that seemed to have been planted over the weekend had vanished from her voice.

"She's not here at the moment. She had to run some errands. Is there something I can do for you?"

Judy studied me. I knew she didn't want me to know about the books she ordered.

"I think I'll just come back when Elaine's here," Judy said and turned to walk out the door.

"I'm sure I can help you," I pushed. "It's kind of my job."

She turned and narrowed her eyes as if studying me. "Did you sign a non-disclosure agreement when you started working here?"

"A non-disclosure agreement about what?"

"To make sure you wouldn't speak of what customers purchase."

I hesitated. Had I signed something like that? I hadn't read through all the paperwork in great detail. "I can assure you, even if I hadn't signed a non-disclosure, I wouldn't say anything about a customer's purchases."

Judy stood there as if considering her options.

"Look, I haven't told anyone about what we spoke of over the weekend, and I don't intend on telling anyone. I assure you, I am no gossip."

"Fine," Judy said, returning to the counter. "I have an order for three books. They're probably labeled Dani Doo."

"Dani Doo?" I asked, trying not to laugh.

"It's obviously a fake name," she said.

Obviously.

I looked under the counter to find three books with post-it notes that said Dani Doo.

"Are these the ones?" I asked. At first glance, the books seemed to be marriage books.

"Yes." She looked toward the door as if someone might walk in at any moment, see the books, and tell the whole town about her marriage problems. "Please put them in a brown paper sack for me."

I rang them up and placed them individually into a sack. Then I realized only two of the books were marriage books. The last one was about depression.

I sucked in a breath. This wasn't my business. Judy wasn't my friend. But I had to ask. It was as if God was nudging me to say something.

"Judy, is this book for you?" I said as gently as I could.

She looked up from her checkbook, and her face paled. For a moment, I thought she might scream at me. Curse me, even. But then tears welled in her eyes as she nodded.

I placed the book in the bag and then stepped out from behind the counter.

"May I pray for you?" I asked.

Judy's eyes were wide. She glanced at the door again.

"It's just the two of us," I said.

She finally nodded.

I placed my hand on her shoulder. "God, You and only You know all that is happening in Judy's life. You are with her every day and every night. I pray You would give her peace. Give her joy. Remove the clouds of depression from her mind, her heart, her soul. Give her energy to keep up with all the things she has going in her life. God, I also pray for Vern. Help him see the treasure he has in Judy. Help them reconnect in unfathomable ways. In Your name I pray, amen."

Judy looked up into my eyes and pulled me into the tightest hug I'd had in a long time. It reminded me of being in the mission field after praying for people who had never heard of Jesus before. How thankful they were to find salvation. Hope.

When she pulled away, my shoulder was damp from her tears.

"Thank you, Clara," she said. She finished signing her check, handed it to me, and walked out of the bookstore without another word.

Mrs. Wilton and Gracie were on the sofa when I walked in that afternoon.

"Hi, Clara," Gracie said in her sweet voice.

"How are you today?" I asked.

"I'm great. Grandma and I have played a hundred games of Candy Land."

From the look on Mrs. Wilton's face, I could believe it.

"Mrs. Wilton, would you like to go lay down for a bit while I take Gracie for some hot cocoa and to see the lights in the square?"

"That would be wonderful," she said. "Nelly won't be home until late, and my energy has run out."

"Leave it to me," I said. "Gracie and I will make dinner when we get back, okay?"

Mrs. Wilton nodded and kissed Gracie on the head before lifting herself off the couch and hobbling to her bedroom. "I love you both," she said over her shoulder.

"We love you too," Gracie and I said in unison.

"Are you really going to take me to get hot cocoa?" Gracie asked.

"I am," I said. "We need to get you bundled up, first.

It's not too cold, but you'll need a jacket, hat, gloves, and boots."

She ran to the door and began putting on her snow clothes while I did the same.

"Where is your mommy?" I asked when we'd gotten outside and were making our way toward the square.

"She went to see a friend," Gracie said with a shrug. "She's been gone all day. Is your brain still broken?"

"It is," I said.

"Then how do you know where we're going? Are you going to be able to get us back to Grandma's house?"

"I grew up in Big Mountain," I said. "I know everything about it."

"Is it called Big Mountain because there's big mountains all around?"

"You're a smart girl," I said. "That's exactly why it's called Big Mountain."

"I like Big Mountain."

"Oh, yeah?"

She nodded as she skipped beside me. "It's so much better than the city."

"I bet the city is nice too."

"Not as nice as here." She waved her arms around. "You can't even see the sky in the city. There's too many buildings."

We turned the corner to the square and made our way to the hot cocoa vendor in the park. I ordered two, and we sat on the bench facing the little shops lining the square.

"This is the best hot cocoa ever," Gracie said as she licked whipped cream from her upper lip. "Can we go see the tree?"

"Definitely."

When we stood, she slipped a gloved hand into mine. Tears stung at my eyes. Was this what it would be like to be a mom?

"Wow." Gracie's eyes sparkled as she looked up at the branches of the tree. "It's beautiful."

"Every year, people who live in Big Mountain bring an ornament to put on the tree."

"Do they get them back?" she asked.

"Yep. They pick them up after Christmas. Or they can donate them to the town. I've put a different ornament on the tree almost every year since I was a baby."

"Which one is yours?" she asked, looking at each ornament carefully but not touching any. She had perfect manners.

"I haven't put one up this year," I said.

"Oh," she said while moving around the tree to see more ornaments.

From across the square, I could see Brian talking to someone. I stopped while Gracie continued slowly around.

It was a woman.

My heart lurched.

It was probably nothing. And even if it was something, it wasn't like I'd exactly jumped at the chance to get back together with him.

I had no claim.

But I couldn't tear my eyes from them.

He had his arm around her shoulders. And then he leaned down and kissed her.

It didn't matter that I was married. It still sucked to see him so close to someone else. I mean, we'd just hung

146

out. He'd just told me he missed me. And here he was kissing some random—

No.

She wasn't random.

She was Nelly.

"Hey Gracie," I said, hurrying around to the other side of the tree. "I think we should go over to the bookstore and get a couple of ornaments to add to the tree. What do you think?"

She smiled, and I knew.

How had I not seen it before?

Her eyes were identical to Brian's.

I sucked in a breath.

"Are we going to go?" she asked, confused by my hesitation.

"Yeah. Yes. Of course."

She took my hand again, and instead of feeling warm and cozy, I felt like an accomplice to a lie.

Did Brian know she was his? Had he lied to me? Or had Nelly lied to him?

"Why don't you pick out one for each of us," I said when we walked into the warmth. I waved at Elaine, who was busy checking out a line of customers.

A small tree sat in the window with ornaments to purchase for the tree in the square. Tourists loved putting ornaments on the tree almost as much as residents.

She took her time examining the ornaments before choosing a little dog and a princess.

"Which one is for me?" I asked when we made our way to the line.

"The princess," she said. "Because you're as pretty as a princess."

Her mother was practically a model, and she thought I was as pretty as a princess.

"And why did you choose a dog for you?"

She looked down at her shoes. "Because I've always wanted a dog," she mumbled. "But we can't have one because we live in an apartment."

I crouched down so our eyes were at the same level. "It's hard wanting something you can't have, isn't it?"

She nodded.

"But sometimes, when we have patience, we get what we've wished for." I didn't know if I was saying this more for her benefit or mine.

She smiled and handed Elaine our ornaments.

"These are great choices," Elaine said to Gracie, then turned to me. "Your mistletoe has been busy tonight."

"Teenagers?" I asked.

"Go see for yourself."

I handed her cash and then walked around a shelf to see Vern and Judy locked in an embrace.

"Surprised?" Elaine said when I returned.

"I thought they—"

"Were having troubles? Yeah, me too."

I smiled. Perhaps my prayer had helped.

"Can we go put the ornaments on the tree now?" Gracie asked.

"Definitely," I said. "See you later, Elaine."

I looked both ways when we exited the shop but saw

no sign of Brian or Nelly. They must have moved on from the square.

I let out a breath of relief. I did not need to be in the middle of this.

Gracie skipped all the way over to the tree, where she carefully placed her dog ornament on the perfect bare branch.

I walked around to the other side to find another empty branch. "I'll be right over here, Gra—oh sorry." I'd walked right into someone.

"It's okay," a man said. "Oh, Clara."

The man was Brian.

He and Nelly stood hand in hand.

"This is Nelly," he said.

"We've met," Nelly said.

"And I have to go," I said. Panic was rising in my chest. In only a matter of seconds, Gracie would walk around the tree looking for me.

"I can explain," Brian said.

"You don't have to. It's okay," I said. I needed to get out of there. "I'm married."

"I think we both realized last night that we weren't right for each other anymore."

Nelly dropped his hand. "You were with *her* last night?"

"I didn't know you were in town. I hadn't heard from you in years." Brian's voice was pleading.

"I'll leave you guys alone to talk about it," I said, turning to leave. But Gracie was there in front of me.

"Are you ready to go?" she asked before she saw her mom behind me. "Hi, Mommy."

Brian's face went white as the falling snow.

Nelly convinced Brian to hear her out then asked me to take Gracie back to Mrs. Wilton's house.

I agreed happily.

"Is that man one of Mommy's friends?" Gracie asked, looking back for the hundredth time.

"I think so, sweetheart," I said. "I liked where you put your ornament. I bet your doggie will be happy there."

"We might not be here to pick him up. I don't know if we're staying for Christmas," she said.

"Would you like me to get him for you after Christmas if you're not here?"

"Yes, please." I couldn't un-see Brian in her eyes.

Mrs. Wilton was still in bed when we arrived.

"Should we cook dinner?" I asked Gracie.

"Can I help?"

"Most definitely."

I'd never cooked with a child before, but she was surprisingly helpful. We made tacos and rice, and by the time we finished, Mrs. Wilton had emerged and was sitting at the table.

"Dinner smells delicious," she said. "Did you make it, Gracie?"

"I helped," she said.

"She helped a lot," I agreed.

"We saw Mommy in the square," Gracie said. "She was with a man."

"She was, was she?" Mrs. Wilton said.

It dawned on me that Mrs. Wilton probably knew about Nelly and Brian's relationship. "Did you know?"

She nodded but didn't elaborate.

I wanted to be upset, but it was impossible to be angry with Mrs. Wilton. Plus, at that very moment, the door opened, and Brian and Nelly walked inside hand-in-hand.

"Gracie, I'd like to introduce you to someone," Nelly said.

Gracie wiped her face and stood up.

Brian glanced at me before crouching down in front of Gracie, holding out a hand. His eyes shone with tears.

"My name is Brian," he said. "It's very nice to meet you."

"Hi, Brian," she said. "Are you Mommy's friend?"

Brian looked at Nelly.

"Yes, sweetheart, he's my friend," Nelly said. "But he's more than that."

"Is he your *boyfriend*?" Gracie said in a teasing tone.

"He used to be," Nelly said. "You know how you haven't ever met your dad?"

Gracie nodded, her eyes widening.

"Well, Brian is your dad," Nelly said.

I shifted in my seat. This felt like an incredibly intimate conversation that I wasn't meant to be part of.

"You're my dad?" Gracie said, examining Brian more closely like she had the ornaments on the Christmas tree.

"I just found out too," he said, but his tone wasn't that of anger. It was of surprised happiness.

"I need to get going for the live nativity," I said, but no one acknowledged me.

CHAPTER 16

*H*ow was it fair that Brian had this perfect little daughter? He hadn't ever said anything about wanting kids. Though he hadn't ever said anything about *not* wanting kids either.

I found myself back in the square, examining my princess ornament.

"A princess. Right," I mumbled to myself. "More like a big fat liar."

My phone vibrated in my pocket.

Lisa.

I should have answered, but I was still angry.

I ignored the call. I'd be seeing her soon enough.

"Hey Clara," a voice called from across the park. "Are you ready for the live nativity?"

I turned to find Hannah jogging toward me.

"Ready as I'll ever be," I said.

"Come on, we have a tent over here with your costume," she said, waving me toward the nativity scene.

The live nativity had been a tradition as old as the town. Residents and tourists alike gathered to hear the sermon and see what hijinks might ensue.

"You're one of the three wise men," Hannah said. "With Lisa and Blake."

She opened the flap to the tent where my two best friends looked at me wide-eyed.

"I tried to call you," Lisa said. "We thought maybe you'd forgotten."

I shrugged. I wasn't going to admit that I didn't want to talk to her.

"Hurry and get changed," Hannah said, not noticing the tension. "We start in five minutes."

I put on my hooded brown robe and followed Blake and Lisa outside.

Devon waved from the podium where he'd be giving the sermon.

I waved back, the butterflies rising again. How long would it take before I no longer loved him?

"Clara?" Brian's voice behind me made me jump.

I turned to find him standing alone with his hands in his pockets.

"I owe you an apology," he said. "I had no idea Nelly was in town, and I had no idea we had a daughter. If I had, I would never have . . ."

"I know," I said, rubbing a hand on his bicep. "It's okay. I'm happy for you. I hope you guys can work it out."

He smiled and pulled me into a hug. "Me too. Thanks, Clara." When he pulled back, he kissed me on the cheek and turned back toward the crowd.

"What was that?" Lisa whispered under her breath when I came to stand next to them.

"Nothing," I said.

And for once, I was telling the truth.

The service began with Sydney's angelic voice. It made me cringe.

I did my best to focus only on being a wise man, staying in character. It was the theme of my life right now. And it was exhausting.

Sydney finished in her usual flash of glory, raising both hands into the sky, a smile on her perfect face.

Devon would be an idiot not to go after her.

"It's such an honor to be here tonight," Devon said, his voice deeper than usual. "I've been waiting to give this sermon since I became a pastor. In fact, I'd prepared a sermon a long time ago just in case I ever got the chance to speak here in the square during the live nativity." He held up his notes. "I must have read over this sermon hundreds of times."

Several people laughed.

"But recently someone very special asked me to consider letting the Holy Spirit speak through me. Instead of practicing, allow God to speak." He looked at the papers in his hands and ripped them directly down the middle.

The crowd gasped.

I could see Judy and Vern standing next to each other near the front. They were smiling.

"So tonight, I will speak from my heart." He finished tearing the pages until the pieces were as small as confetti. "If you didn't know, my wife was recently in a car accident. We had a huge argument—yes, we fight."

More laughter.

"And she got into the car."

The laughter stopped.

He looked down at the tiny pieces of paper firmly pinched between his finger and thumb.

"And because of me—because of my stubbornness, because of my harsh words—she could have died." He paused for a few seconds.

"But she didn't," he whispered. "She didn't die. She's still with us today."

Several people turned to look at me. I turned my gaze on the baby Jesus doll lying in the hay-filled cradle.

"And as ashamed as I am to say this, I was almost happy she'd lost her memory. That I might get a second chance to woo the love of my life."

Tears sprung to my eyes. I was the love of his life. He wanted me. And I was being selfish and awful.

I needed to tell him the truth. Good or bad, I needed to come clean. He deserved honesty.

"But then I realized maybe she wouldn't want me."

I looked up at him, but he wasn't looking in my direction. It was almost as if he were avoiding looking my way.

"But what does this mean for you?" he asked. "I don't know. I've been trying and trying to find purpose in this. Trying to gain insight. I mean, I'm God's child, right? I have a relationship with Him, right? I talk to Him every single day. And yet, He's been silent."

Snow started falling in small flakes.

"I don't know how to navigate this area of my life. Never once did I think my marriage would be compromised. Besides God's love, that was the most solid truth in my life. And now, I don't know what's true. Maybe I'm angry. No, scratch that. I am angry. And that's okay. God can take it.

"As I look out into the crowd tonight, I know some of you are angry with God too. Some of you have become so angry, you've turned your back on Him." He wiped a snowflake from his nose. "Let me tell you, He still loves you. Just like I know, He still loves me.

"My sermon today was going to be about how God doesn't break down the door to your heart—a sermon I recently gave in my church. I was going to equate it to how I'm trying to give my wife the option to love me again. To show her how much I love her. But every time I do something out of the ordinary—something I would have done when we were courting—I feel this immense amount of guilt. I should have done those things while she still remembered me, and maybe we wouldn't be in this position. But instead, I've been trying to break down the door to her heart.

"But it's not working." His gaze rested directly on me. "None of this is working. She might never remember me. She might end up with someone else, and there's nothing I can do about it."

He threw the confetti pieces of his sermon in the air.

"So tonight, I'm going to ask you to let God in." He looked back to the crowd with a smile. "Celebrate Jesus' birth by giving Him your love. Celebrate His life by loving your neighbor. And above all, don't take those you love for granted."

I didn't sing when Sydney retook the stage and sang one final song, ending with a prayer of hope and love. I stood like a statue as people walked by, their gazes like lasers of judgment.

Eventually, the live nativity was over. I wasn't sure if I didn't have feeling in my extremities because of the temperature drop or because of the effect Devon's words had on me. Was he really giving up on me? On us?

The park was empty when I emerged from the tent after changing out of the costume. I'd managed to avoid Lisa and Blake in the commotion. The only thing on my mind was finding Devon and telling him the truth. Whether he forgave me or not, he needed to know.

His car was still parked in the square, but I couldn't find him anywhere.

I walked around the Christmas tree, my gaze pulled to my princess ornament. I hadn't acted like much of a princess lately.

Then I heard a voice on the other side of the tree—Sydney's voice.

"I can't believe she would do that to you," she said.

I peeked around to find her standing ridiculously close to Devon.

"She doesn't remember me, Sydney. Of course, she would. She thinks she's single, and he's the last man she remembers."

"But she *knows* she's married to you."

Tears streaked down Devon's face while Sydney rubbed his back.

I wanted to—needed to—tell Sydney to get away from my husband. But I couldn't. Something in me wanted to hear what they were going to say. What he was going to say.

"I know you don't understand this, but being married is challenging," Devon said.

"Maybe someday, I will." She moved slightly closer—their bodies almost touching.

Devon looked over at her and their eyes locked. "Sydney, I think I need to be alone."

"Someone needs to be here for you," she said.

Devon looked torn. Was he seriously not going to walk away?

Sydney rested her head on his shoulder.

His eyes widened with shock. But he didn't move.

My throat went dry.

"Clara?" Gracie called from behind me.

Sydney's head shot up as she and Devon looked straight at me.

For a split second, I stood frozen. Devon's eyes pleaded. But I couldn't deal with this. Who knows how far it would have gone if Gracie hadn't interrupted.

I turned and walked away from them.

"There you are," Nelly said as she, Brian, Gracie, and Mrs. Wilton stood from their benches.

"Do you want to get some hot cocoa with us?" Gracie asked, her voice excited.

I swiped the tears from my eyes. "Sure, kiddo."

"What's wrong?" Mrs. Wilton asked. "You look like you just saw the Ghost of Christmas Past."

"Clara, wait," Devon said from behind me. "It's not what you think."

"What's not what she thinks?" Brian asked, moving to stand beside me, his hand still firmly in Nelly's.

"This has nothing to do with you," Devon said.

"If it has something to do with Clara, it has something to do with me." Brian's jaw was set in a hard line as if daring Devon to take a swing. "She's my friend."

"Just your friend?" Devon's voice was full of accusation.

Who was he to be accusing anyone of anything when he was the one who was all snuggly with Sydney only moments before?

"What's that supposed to mean?" Brian asked.

"I saw you kissing her before my sermon," Devon said.

Nelly gasped and yanked her hand from Brian's. "You were *kissing* her?"

"I haven't kissed her in years," Brian said.

I nodded in agreement, unable to find my voice.

"Maybe what you saw was me kissing her—*on the cheek* —in thanks for being so cool about Nelly and I getting back together."

"Who's Nelly?" Devon asked, his tone more hesitant.

"I'm Nelly." Nelly stepped forward. "And this is my daughter—our daughter—" she looked at Brian with a smile and then reached for Gracie's hand "—Gracie."

Devon's face went as red as a tomato.

"Nelly, dear," Mrs. Wilton said from behind us. "I don't fe—"

But before she could finish the sentence, she had fallen to the ground.

CHAPTER 17

I hadn't realized the crowd we'd elicited, but the moment Mrs. Wilton fell, it was as if the entire park was around us.

Brian leaped into action. "Devon, call 9-1-1." His fingers were on Mrs. Wilton's neck. "She has a pulse, but it's weak. We need to get her to the hospital."

Gracie was crying crocodile tears as she knelt at her grandmother's side. Nelly wiped tears from her eyes as she tried to comfort her daughter.

I knelt next to Mrs. Wilton and took her hand in mine.

"God, please let her be okay," I whispered repeatedly.

Devon knelt beside me and rubbed my back, whispering prayers.

"I'm sorry about my behavior at the park," Devon said. "I should never have put myself in that position with Sydney. And I never should have accused you of doing anything inappropriate with Brian. That was jealousy talking, and I let it affect my entire night."

We were following the ambulance at a distance since we couldn't legally go as fast as it could. Plus, the roads were snow-packed. The last thing we needed to do was get into another accident.

"It's okay," I said.

He wasn't the one who should have been apologizing. It should have been me.

But now didn't seem like the right time to communicate what I'd done. My brain was too jumbled with worry.

"Do you think Mrs. Wilton will be okay?" I asked.

"All we can do is pray," Devon said. It was his automatic pastor answer. "I'm sorry. That probably doesn't help you feel any better."

"It's okay. You're right. Praying is really all we can do."

They had hurried Mrs. Wilton into the emergency room when we got there.

"What happened?" Blake asked.

I let Devon answer their questions.

"She just passed out," Devon said. "They didn't tell us what happened."

"It's probably her heart," Nelly said. She was sitting between Brian and Gracie.

"What do you mean, it was probably her heart?" Lisa asked. Uncharacteristic dark bags hung under her eyes.

"That's why I'm here," Nelly said. "She called and told me she didn't have much time left. That she wanted to spend it with Gracie and me."

Lisa. Blake, and I exchanged looks.

"Did you know?" Blake asked me.

"No," I said.

"Why wouldn't she have told us?" Lisa asked Nelly.

"She didn't want to disrupt your lives," Nelly said.

How selfish was I that I hadn't noticed even when I'd moved in with her? I was so tangled up in my own life, my stupid problems, and this idiotic lie I didn't see her deteriorating before my very eyes.

"I'm going to take a walk," I said.

"Do you want some company?" Devon asked.

"I think I just need to be alone for a while." I smiled. "But, thanks."

The brisk winter air hit my lungs when I walked out into the parking lot. Carolers sang in the distance, a song about peace and joy.

I'd really messed up my peace and joy this year.

"Clara?" Brian's voice came from behind me. "Mrs. Wilton wants to see you."

I whipped around. "Me? Why me?"

He shrugged. "Nelly and Gracie are already in there, but she specifically asked for you."

I followed him back into the hospital and past the questioning looks of my friends and my husband.

"I don't know how long she has, so prepare yourself," Brian said as he opened the door to a room.

"Clara." The frailty in Mrs. Wilton's voice brought tears to my eyes. "Come sit."

Nelly and Gracie walked past me and joined Brian in the hall.

I sat on the edge of her bed, and she took my hand in hers. "I'm sorry I didn't tell you girls."

I could only nod, afraid my voice would be replaced with loud sobs. Tears ran down my cheeks.

"But I love you too much to see you ruin your own life," she said. "This charade has to end."

"I know," I managed.

"You have to tell the people you love the truth. They'll either forgive you or they won't, but you can't live a lie. The truth about lying is that it will tear you up inside."

"I know," I said again.

"I love you so much, my dear. And even though my time here is short, I'll always be with you."

Now I was sobbing. I wrapped my arms around her neck, knowing this was probably the last time I'd do so. "I love you too," I said into her shoulder. "Thank you for always being there for me—for us. I'm really going to miss you."

"That's enough blubbering over this little old lady." She squeezed me one last time. "Now go get Lisa and Blake."

I stood and took one last look at the woman who had been a fixture in my life for so many years. "I love you."

"I love you too, my dear."

Devon and I sat side by side alone in the waiting room. It was now or never.

"Devon, I need to tell you something." I turned my body toward him.

"I'm all ears."

"And please, just let me talk. It will be hard enough to say what I need to."

He nodded once.

"I lied," I said, the words tumbling out of my mouth. I looked down at my jeans. "I never had amnesia."

When I looked back up into his eyes, I couldn't tell whether he was angry, hurt, or both. His face was blank.

"When we had that fight, I just wanted to give up. I wanted a divorce. I was so tired of trying to be someone I wasn't—the perfect pastor's wife. I never wanted to be a pastor's wife. I'm not good enough to be one. And then you confirmed exactly that."

I sucked in a breath.

"You told me I wasn't doing good enough, even though I was trying with all I had." I tucked a stray piece of hair behind my ear. "At least I thought I was trying with all I had."

It was even harder to say the next words.

"I was so bitter about losing control of my life, losing control of my identity, and not getting what I wanted— children primarily—that I think I rebelled by not doing my best at things. I pretended I was doing my best, but my heart was angry, and that came out in the way I did everything."

The tears began welling up again.

"And then when I got into that accident—and no, it wasn't intentional—I figured this was the perfect way for us both to get what we wanted. Or what I thought we wanted. You could still be a pastor, because who would fault you for divorcing a woman who didn't remember you? And I could stop pretending to be someone I'm not. I could adopt a baby and become a mother like I had always wanted.

"And then you were so nice and sweet, and everything got so jumbled up."

He sat as still as a statue.

"And I understand if you never forgive me. And we don't have to tell anyone else that my amnesia was fake—is fake—so you can still be a pastor, and you can even marry Sydney if you want."

This elicited a pshh sound from him, which made me feel the tiniest bit better.

"But I would like you to forgi—"

"Devon?" Brian said from behind me.

We both looked back at him.

"Mrs. Wilton is asking to speak with you," he said. "Something about getting right with God."

I smiled. "We can talk about this later."

He stood hesitantly with a strange look on his face as if he wanted to tell me something, but instead, he just shook his head and followed Brian back.

Even though I was ninety-nine percent sure Devon might never speak to me again, I felt an enormous weight lifted off my shoulders. At least he knew.

I'm so sorry, God, for lying.

Before Lisa, Blake, Nelly, or anyone else could return to the waiting room, I left the hospital and called a taxi.

166

*I*t didn't feel right to stay at Mrs. Wilton's anymore, knowing she would probably never return.

By the time I had my things packed and the room tidied, a text appeared across my screen from Nelly.

She's gone.

The two words I knew were coming still stole my breath away.

A taxi waited for me at the curb when I emerged. The stars sparkled in the dark sky.

When I told the taxi driver the address, he gave me a funny look.

"Don't worry. It's a cabin."

"In the national forest?"

"It was grandfathered into my family," I assured him. "The road will have been cleared."

He shrugged and put the car in gear.

I made a fire as quickly as possible in the old wood fireplace and curled up on the dusty couch with my favorite old quilt as I watched the sunrise shade the forest a pretty pink.

Exhaustion eventually took over, lulling me to the soundest sleep I'd had in weeks.

I probably would have slept until Christmas if it hadn't been for a loud knocking at the door around noon.

I wiped the sleep from my eyes and stretched my arms overhead. The cabin had finally warmed up, but the fire was dying. I added another log before answering the insistent pounding from outside.

Blake and Lisa stood shivering on the other side of the door.

"Can we come in?" Blake asked.

"Sure," I said.

"It's so warm in here," Lisa said, pulling a blanket over her and sitting in the rocking chair.

"Fire," I said stupidly. Of course, it was because of the fire.

"Before Mrs. Wilton passed," Lisa said in her stay-strong-for-everyone voice, "she asked Blake and me to forgive you."

Blake settled in next to me on the couch. I covered us both with the quilt.

"What was she talking about?" Blake asked. "Did you do something with Brian?"

Anger flared up inside of me, but I pushed it down. Now wasn't the time to let my pride win. Now was the time to come clean.

"I'm sorry I left the hospital when Isla was born the way I did," I said. "That was incredibly rude and inconsiderate."

Neither of them spoke.

"And to answer your question," I continued. "No, I didn't do anything with Brian. We went on what you might call a date, but it ended in my realizing we're just too different from one another now."

"You mean he's too different from you, right?" Blake asked.

"And I'm too different from him." I glanced down at my hands in my lap. I felt like my entire body was shaking. "I—" My voice cracked. "I never had amnesia."

The room was silent. None of us moved.

When I finally glanced up, both of my friends' mouths were open in shock.

"I know," I said. "I lied. To you. To Devon. And that's what I want to ask you to forgive me for."

"Mrs. Wilton knew this entire time?" Blake asked.

"I didn't even tell her," I said. "She knew the moment I walked into her apartment."

"But why would you do that?" I could tell by the tone of Blake's voice she was hurt.

"So she could get a divorce," Lisa answered for me. "Right?"

I looked back down at my hands.

"The night of the accident, when you called me, I

should have talked to you," Lisa said. "Then maybe you wouldn't have done this."

"I didn't do it intentionally," I said. "I mean, I pretended to have amnesia intentionally, but the car accident was just that—an accident."

"Does Devon know?" Blake asked.

"I told him last night at the hospital," I said.

"What did he say?" Lisa asked.

"He didn't say anything," I said. "Brian called him in to talk to Mrs. Wilton before he had a chance to respond."

I sucked in a breath.

"I know it was wrong, but I felt like Devon tricked me," I said, my voice barely audible over the crackling fire. "He never told me he wanted to be a pastor. And then when I told him I didn't want to do it anymore, he told me I didn't have a choice. I was tired of being his servant. I deserve to be happy too. To have a career that I love. To have—" my voice caught "—children."

Neither spoke.

"I know you don't understand. Both of you have babies. Beautiful, wonderful, adorable babies. And husbands who want babies. I want to be a mommy. I want to be part of your mommy club so we can all talk about things and go to mommy groups together."

Tears rolled off my chin. I brushed them away with my sleeve. "I'm sorry I lied. I feel terrible, but I didn't know what other option I had. If I had knowingly divorced him, he would have lost both his wife and his church. This way, he would only lose his wife."

"Do you think he'd choose the church over you?" Lisa asked.

I shrugged. "I'm not sure I want to know the answer to that question. But I know God called him to be a pastor. I trust that's true."

"Don't you think God called him to be your husband too?" Lisa asked. "And for you to be his wife?"

Why did she have to make everything more difficult?

"And do you think maybe you're not exactly the person you were the moment you married Devon?" Lisa asked. "People change. Circumstances change. Jobs change. And when you married him, you signed up for it all. No matter what."

"I don't think he meant to trick you," Blake said. "He never knew you didn't want to be a pastor's wife."

"I didn't know I had to tell him," I said. "Should I tell him I don't want to be the wife of a bull rider? A carney? A male stripper?"

"I don't know that I'd put male stripper and pastor in the same category," Blake said with a small laugh.

"Yeah, because at least as a male stripper's wife, I wouldn't have to go door-to-door, begging people to come to his strip club."

Blake snorted and dissolved into a fit of laughter. Lisa and I weren't far behind.

I leaned over and put my head on Blake's shoulder.

When the laughter had stopped, I looked at my friends. "Will you forgive me for lying to you?"

"Of course we will," Blake said.

"Absolutely forgiven," Lisa said. "Now, let's get this cabin ready for Christmas, shall we?"

"What do you mean?" I asked.

Lisa stood up and opened the door where Nathan and Dan stood with a tree and a bunch of boxes.

"What about the kids?" I asked.

"Hannah's babysitting," Blake said. "She just couldn't wait to get her hands on Isla."

I hugged them. "Thank you for your forgiveness."

CHAPTER 19

*C*hristmas was there before I knew it. I'd spent the rest of the week at the cabin, enjoying the peace and quiet.

Colorful lights twinkled from every window frame. The tree stood between the living room and the kitchen with blue and silver ornaments dangling from the branches. An angel completed the look as she sat majestically on top of the tree as if watching over me.

All bundled up, I jumped into a taxi to get to church. Devon hadn't called or texted since we'd spoken at the hospital. Whether I was going to church because it was a tradition, or to see Devon, didn't matter. I'd be there.

The candlelight service was the most popular service of the year, and it was the first time in our church I didn't have a role to play in making sure it all went off without a hitch. I showed up just before the song service began so I didn't have to talk to anyone. I wasn't sure if Devon had told anyone or not, but I didn't want to take any chances.

I'd happily face the jury just as soon as Christmas was over.

Sydney was nowhere to be found and, for a moment, I wondered if she and Devon were somewhere together. I pushed the thought away and sang along with the children's choir.

When Devon stepped on stage, he seemed happy. Unencumbered by emotion. It made me equally happy and sad. Happy because he was happy, sad because he was happy without me. He only spoke for a couple of minutes, finishing with a Christmas prayer before we sang one last song.

I returned my candle to a volunteer I'd never seen before and scanned the lobby for Devon. Disappointment welled up within me when I couldn't find him anywhere. I hadn't spent a Christmas without him since we met. My new normal wasn't exactly as freeing as I'd imagined.

Reluctantly, I left the church and walked into the park to the tree. I had a promise to keep.

Nelly, Brian, and Gracie had returned to New York with Brian's parents for Christmas. Nelly sent a text telling us we'd have a celebration of life for Mrs. Wilton in the coming months.

The little dog ornament sat on the same branch Gracie had chosen. I decided to leave the princess ornament for the town to keep, but Gracie needed her dog.

"You know you're not supposed to take those until after Christmas."

I spun around, dog in hand, and began to explain. "I—I need—"

It was Devon.

"Oh, hi," I said.

"Hi."

"I had to get this for Gracie," I said. "I promised."

He smiled.

"How are you?" I asked.

"I've been better," he said. "But I've been worse."

"I figured you'd still be talking to people." I motioned over at the church.

"There's only one person I want to talk to."

My heart leaped. Had he forgiven me?

"I wanted to give you your Christmas gift," he said, pulling a small flat box from his pocket.

"I have a gift for you, too." I thought about the tie that he would probably hate but that kept my charade afloat. "But not with me."

"That's okay." He looked at the box in my hand. "Don't open it yet. Let's go on a walk."

We walked side-by-side toward the diner, where I assumed he'd want to have dinner. But before we got there, he stopped me.

"Okay, open it," he said. His eyes glittered.

I pulled the top off the box to find a key. "Is this for my car?" I asked. It didn't look like a car key, but maybe they had to change the starter thing or something.

"Not for your car," he said.

I searched him for a hint. Was it a metaphor? The key to his heart? The thought was too presumptuous to say aloud.

"I don't know. I'm sorry," I said.

He grabbed my shoulders and turned me ninety degrees.

My childhood home was all lit up across the street. A beautiful Christmas tree sat in the bay window, and lights wrapped around the pillars on the front porch.

"I don't understand," I said. "Did you?"

My heart raced. Was he telling me what I thought he was telling me?

"I bought it," he said. "Before the accident. I wanted it to be a surprise."

Tears sprung to my eyes, my heart swelling with so much undeserved love. "Can we go inside?"

Devon nodded. "But first, I have to tell you something."

I turned toward him.

"I knew you were lying," he said.

"You knew?" I asked. "The whole time?"

"Since we had dinner at the apartment. You moved around the kitchen as if it was yours. Which it was, of course."

"Why didn't you say something?"

"Because I also knew why you were doing it." He sighed. "I wanted so badly to push myself onto you. To call you out and demand we go back to the way it was. The church was suffering. Without you, it felt so empty and so disorganized. It made me see how much you really did."

I was stunned. He knew the entire time.

"I bought this house before you brought up the idea of kids. And when you did, I panicked. I thought we'd talk about it more once I'd surprised you with the house. I shouldn't have gotten irritated, though. And if you'll have me back, I'll do everything in my power not to take you for granted again."

"Does that mean you forgive me?"

"I'd forgiven you the moment I knew. You may have been the one who lied about the amnesia, but I'm the one who drove you to the lie. I didn't give you any other option."

"Lying shouldn't have been my first instinct," I said.

"It wasn't. You tried to talk to me about it. You said no. I pushed and pushed because I knew I could count on you like I can't count on anyone else."

"But what about Sydney?"

"What about Sydney?"

"When I saw you the other night, it looked like there might have been something developing there."

"I let Sydney go the next day. I realized how inappropriate she had been acting. My mind had been so focused on you that I hadn't bothered to see how her behavior was toxic for the church."

"The church," I whispered. "What will the church think when they find out? I'm assuming we're not going to keep this a secret and pretend my memory came back."

"The board already knows. They're meeting about it after Christmas."

"What if they let you go?" I asked.

"Then they let me go. You're more important to me than the church. And, assuming we agree to it, I could always start another church someday."

"I'm so sorry I put you in this position. It was selfish and unkind."

"And it may have saved our marriage," he said. "That is if you'll have me back."

I wrapped my arms around him and kissed him the way we kissed when we were first married.

"I assume that's a yes?" He laughed.

"Yes, of course, I'll have you back," I said. "Now, let's go check out our house."

When we walked inside, my mom, dad, and brothers sat on the couches in the living room. The smell of my mom's famous pot roast hit my nose and made my mouth water.

"I thought you guys were on your cruise," I said.

"And miss Christmas with you?" Dad stood up and hugged me. "Not a chance."

The rest of them hugged me.

"What do you think about Devon buying you this house?" Mom said.

"I couldn't be happier," I said. "I'm so sorry I lied to you."

"You didn't lie to us," Dad said. "We weren't even here."

"Still, it was wrong."

"Well, we forgive you," Mom said. "Now, should we take a tour before we eat?"

"A tour?" I asked.

"There's only one room I want to show you," Devon said, taking my hand in his and leading me up the stairs. If he led me into the master bedroom in front of my entire family, I might never get over the embarrassment. But instead of turning left at the top of the stairs, he turned right to the door where my bedroom used to be.

"Did you make it up to look like my childhood bedroom or something?" I asked, nervous about what I'd find on the other side.

"Not exactly." Devon opened the door to the most beautiful nursery I'd ever seen in my life. A round crib sat directly in the middle of the room with a small silver chandelier hanging above. Giant stuffed animals sat off to the side as if waiting for the day I'd place my very own baby on the soft mattress.

A plush rocking chair with matching footstool sat in the window—the place where I'd rock my tiny baby day and night.

"We can add bits of color depending on whether we have a girl or a boy, but I wanted to get the basics, at least."

I'd never cried so much as I had in the past week. Tears of joy and hope escaped my eyes.

"Thank you," I said, hugging him. "Thank you so much."

"Anything for you," he said.

"Okay, you're making me weepy," Mom said. "Let's get some food."

The boys cheered and ran down the stairs like old times.

I took one last look at the room I'd get to raise my babies in. The room I, myself, was raised in.

Thank you, God, for your unending grace.

CHAPTER 20

*T*he board met for what felt like hours. Devon and I had prayed and prayed for the right solution. Not necessarily the right one for us, but the right one for the church, for God.

"No matter what, we've always got each other," Devon said for the hundredth time that day.

I squeezed his hand.

Finally, the door of the boardroom opened, and Judy walked out. "Can you please come inside?"

I looked at Devon, and he shrugged. Neither of us had expected to see Judy in attendance.

And since she was, it was unlikely we would be able to stay at the church.

"First, I'd like to thank both of you for your honesty," Vern said when we sat down. "We know no one is perfect. We all make mistakes."

Did that mean they would forgive us?

Please, God, let them forgive us. Let Devon keep his—our— Your—church.

"But pastors are called to a higher set of standards."

My gaze dropped to my hands in my lap. That didn't sound good.

"As a pastor, you're supposed to be the example, the leader. And several of the board members believe this incident might taint your image in the eyes of our congregation."

Devon nodded beside me, his face unnaturally calm. He had more faith than the entire board put together.

"But those members are in the minority."

My head shot up.

"We asked Judy to come in because she's been one of your biggest critics from day one. If anyone had a reason to fire you, she'd find it." Vern reached out, and Judy took his hand. They smiled at each other. "And she gave a testimony that changed those board members' minds."

What was he talking about?

"You see, Judy and I have been caught in a lie ourselves recently. And although I am not the pastor of this church, I still believe I should be held to a high standard because I am on the board.

"Judy confided in Clara that our marriage was basically over."

Devon looked at me, surprise in his eyes.

"We would come to church every week, acting as if we were in love, as if everything was all right. And then we'd get home and not speak to one another all week. And if we did speak, look out." He and Judy laughed, but everyone else sat in silence. "Until Clara prayed for Judy."

Vern poked a finger into the corner of his eye and wiped it on his pants, his voice now thick with emotion.

"You see. I wasn't being the husband God called me to be. But since that day, Judy and I have been going to counseling and working to repair the damage that has been done.

"Once Judy told that story, we were all able to open up about how flawed we really are." Vern looked around at the other board members. "Being a pastor doesn't mean you're perfect. And we all agreed that we'd much prefer a pastor who can admit to being imperfect over one who pretends to be perfect."

"Does that mean we get to stay?" I asked.

"As I understand it, the reason you did all this was because you didn't want to stay," Vern said. "Am I correct?"

I nodded.

"Then we will leave it up to the two of you. We don't want a pastor here whose wife despises the church."

"Please say you'll stay," Judy said, her eyes misting.

I glanced at Devon. His arm went around my shoulder, and he pulled me close.

"Yes," I whispered, my throat tight with love for both Devon and what we could grow toward together.

"Yes," Devon echoed. "We'll stay."

As Devon's kiss pressed against the top of my head, warmth flooded my soul. I tilted my head to meet his gaze. "There's no place I'd rather be."

And that was the truth.

Thank you so much for reading *The Truth About Lying*. If

you enjoyed the book, please leave a review on Amazon, Goodreads, or any of your favorite retailers.

I'd love it if you'd join my email list! Sign up at

http://bit.ly/2ObgAwb

to get exclusive information on upcoming book releases and events.

ACKNOWLEDGMENTS

As always, I thank God first. Thank You for giving me the gift of telling stories.

To my family, thank you for reading my books and listening to me talk about them obsessively.

To those of you who managed to beta read this book in the middle of the summer, thank you. Your input is invaluable.

And to my readers, I appreciate you so much!

ABOUT THE AUTHOR

Crystal Ferry loves Hallmark movies, chocolate, and all things Christmas. When she's not wrangling her four kids and four dogs, you'll find her with her laptop crafting stories.

Connect with Crystal on Facebook or email:
CrystalFerryAuthor@gmail.com

CPSIA information can be obtained
at www.ICGtesting.com
Printed in the USA
LVHW111455050722
722773LV00006B/565

9 780999 602188